They made it to the bedroom at last

Lying with her head on Jason's chest, Heather listened to the evenness of his breathing and waited for sleep to claim her.

They'd shared something tonight that ran deeper than a casual encounter. He'd felt it, too, she was certain.

She tried not to think about what might happen as a result. Perhaps, this time, there wouldn't be any emotional fallout. Surely she hadn't misjudged Jason's capacity for intimacy.

A momentary uneasiness disturbed her tranquillity. They'd forgotten to take precautions. What if something came of it?

A longing jolted through her. A baby. To nurture a child through the miraculous stages of growth would be a joy almost as great as finding the love of her life.

As sleep began to claim her and she snuggled closer to Jason, Heather wondered whether it was possible that she might have both.

Dear Reader,

This month Harlequin American Romance delivers favorite authors and irresistible stories of heart, home and happiness that are sure to leave you smiling.

COWBOYS BY THE DOZEN, Tina Leonard's new family-connected miniseries, premieres this month with *Frisco Joe's Fiancée*, in which a single mother and her daughter give a hard-riding, heartbreaking cowboy second thoughts about bachelorhood.

Next, in *Prognosis: A Baby? Maybe*, the latest book in Jacqueline Diamond's THE BABIES OF DOCTORS CIRCLE miniseries, a playboy doctor's paternal instincts and suspicions are aroused when he sees a baby girl with the woman who had shared a night of passion with him. Was this child his? THE HARTWELL HOPE CHESTS, Rita Herron's delightful series, resumes with *Have Cowboy, Need Cupid*, in which a city girl suddenly starts dreaming about a cowboy groom after opening an heirloom hope chest. And rounding out the month is *Montana Daddy*, a reunion romance and secret baby story by Charlotte Maclay.

Enjoy this month's offerings as Harlequin American Romance continues to celebrate its yearlong twentieth anniversary.

Melissa Jeglinski
Associate Senior Editor
Harlequin American Romance

PROGNOSIS: A BABY? MAYBE

Jacqueline Diamond

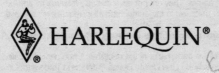

HARLEQUIN®

TORONTO • NEW YORK • LONDON
AMSTERDAM • PARIS • SYDNEY • HAMBURG
STOCKHOLM • ATHENS • TOKYO • MILAN • MADRID
PRAGUE • WARSAW • BUDAPEST • AUCKLAND

This book is dedicated to Marcia Holman with thanks
for her friendship and her expert advice.

ISBN 0-373-16978-7

PROGNOSIS: A BABY? MAYBE

ABOUT THE AUTHOR

The daughter of a doctor and an artist, Jacqueline Diamond claims to have researched the field of obstetrics primarily by developing a large range of complications during her pregnancies. She's also lucky enough to have a friend and neighbor who's an obstetrical nurse. The author of more than sixty novels, Jackie lives in Southern California with her husband and two sons. She loves to hear from readers. You can write to her at P.O. Box 1315, Brea, CA 92822, or by e-mail at JDiamondfriends@aol.com.

Books by Jacqueline Diamond

HARLEQUIN AMERICAN ROMANCE

*The Babies of Doctors Circle

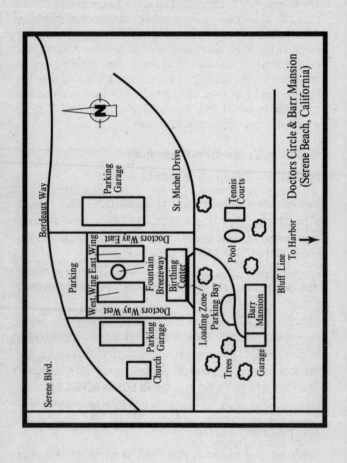

Doctors Circle & Barr Mansion
(Serene Beach, California)

Chapter One

The last man in the world that Heather Rourke wanted to see stood in the doorway of her office. She glanced up questioningly, trying to mask her speeding pulse with an air of cool professional detachment.

"Now that we're going to be colleagues, Doctor, I hope we can put the past behind us," said Jason Carmichael.

Green ice, that's what had formed his eyes in some glacial age when Neanderthals stalked the world, Heather thought. In this case, the Neanderthal had a degree from Harvard Medical School, short dark hair and a lean build beneath his expensive business suit. His collected manner failed to assuage her opinion that he was a semi-savage male who probably ate his steak sandwiches raw.

"As far as I'm concerned, there is no past," Heather told the new head of the Infertility Clinic.

The latest addition to the Doctors Circle complex, the clinic was in the final stages of remodeling and would open officially in April, two months from now. Jason had arrived earlier this week but had been so busy that, until now, he and Heather had exchanged only brief, impersonal greetings. She wished they could keep it that way.

Ever since his appointment had been announced last fall, rumors had spread about her supposed dislike of him. They'd been right.

Some fellow staffers attributed Heather's attitude to professional jealousy. Since she'd worked as an obstetrician at Doctors Circle for three years and had handled most of the infertility cases, she might have expected to be promoted to the post.

Others guessed that there was some personal conflict in their backgrounds. No one knew the truth, that she'd nearly made love to this man more than a year ago after meeting him at a convention. What a disaster that had been!

Heather hadn't confided the story even to the few friends with whom she'd shared her other secret, that she'd given up a baby for adoption when she was fifteen. Although her daughter had reappeared in her life and, along with a baby granddaughter, was now very dear to her, Heather saw no reason to spread that information around Doctors Circle. In her opinion, the more private she kept her life, the better.

"Did you get my e-mail?" Jason said. "I expected a reply by now."

"I'm not sure. Which e-mail was that?"

"I've only sent one."

"Then no, I haven't seen it," Heather said.

Jason gritted his teeth. "I don't see how you could have missed it. I sent it twice."

"I'm sure it's in the queue." She gestured at the computer screen that dominated the scattering of files and medication samples on her desk. "I clear it every Friday." Today was Wednesday.

Annoyance twisted his mouth. "You'll find I'm a stickler for organization, Doctor. That includes keeping up with your messages."

"I'm a stickler for being on time with my patients, even when that leaves me with a messy desk." Heather checked her watch. "Why don't you simply tell me what the message said? And why don't we drop this 'doctor' nonsense and call each other by our first names?"

Judging by his frown, Jason wasn't accustomed to being addressed so cavalierly. He'd better get used to it. People in Serene Beach, California, didn't stand on ceremony. Especially her.

"Very well, *Heather*." He emphasized her name. "I wrote to suggest that you and I walk through the new facility, unfinished as it is. I'd like to consult you about our planning."

A blush heated her cheeks. With her short mop of red curls and sprinkle of freckles, Heather colored easily when embarrassed.

And she *was* embarrassed. She'd been giving Jason a hard time when all he'd wanted was to discuss the plans for the clinic. Although she hated paperwork and therefore hadn't coveted the post of department head, she did want a say in how they set up staffing and scheduling.

So far, the two of them were the only doctors assigned to the clinic, although others would be arriving soon. His request was an appropriate professional courtesy.

"My four o'clock staff meeting got canceled. I could join you then," she said. "Would that work?"

"Certainly." Jason cleared his throat. "Listen, that isn't the only thing I wanted to discuss. We have some unfinished business to clear up."

Uh-oh. "Which business would that be?"

"Atlanta," he said.

Heather definitely did not want to discuss the medical convention in Georgia where they'd met some fifteen months earlier. That unpleasant experience was best consigned to the scrap heap of memories.

What on earth had possessed her to go up to his room and throw her inhibitions out the window? Thank goodness he'd fallen asleep before they could consummate a passion that, in retrospect, struck her as incomprehensible. His crankiness the following day had made it evident what a close call she'd had.

"That business is finished. You dotted the i's and crossed the t's very succinctly the next morning." She closed the file she'd been reviewing.

"I wasn't at my best that Friday," Jason said. If she hadn't known him better, it might have sounded like an apology.

"Being hungover is no excuse for rudeness."

"I can be difficult when I have a headache," he said. "Who isn't?"

"You must get a lot of headaches. You're famous for your curt manner." Heather lifted her coffee cup, discovered that it was empty and set it down again. "You reduced your secretary to tears yesterday, I heard."

Usually, the efficiency of the grapevine at Doctors Circle drove Heather crazy. Once in a while, however, it came in handy.

"I didn't expect her to react so strongly." Jason ducked his head, and a well-shaped head it was, too, for a Neanderthal, she reluctantly conceded. "By the time I arrived, Coral had already unpacked all my files from Virginia. I suppose I overreacted, but she'll have to repack everything when we move across the courtyard to our new quarters."

"You're the one who requested a secretary be hired

before you got here. In any case, you could have sent her instructions, since you're obviously a whiz with e-mail." Heather got to her feet.

"I assumed she would liaise with my secretary in Virginia," Jason said.

Heather decided it would be impolitic to mention how much she hated trendy words like *liaise*. "Coral's new and I am sure she was trying to make a good impression."

"I hope she'll learn not to take things so personally." He shrugged. "I get so focused on my work, I don't always realize the impact of what I'm saying."

"By the way, I believe Edith Krick has been assigned as your nurse. You'll like her. She's highly competent and she has a thick hide where cranky doctors are concerned." Heather started for the doorway, but Jason was blocking her path.

Should she elbow him out of the way? Try to sidle past? The prospect of brushing against him sent an unwanted tremor through Heather.

She didn't like being attracted to this man. It had been a big mistake the first time they met, and she never repeated a mistake if she could help it.

"Who did Edith work with before?" Jason asked, apparently unaware of her desire to exit the room. Typical of him to be clueless, she thought.

"An obstetrician who left last fall. I could tell you all about his divorce and why he decided to move to Connecticut, but I won't. The story is as long as your arm."

"Thank you. There are enough people gossiping around here already, I've gathered." The man smiled. Heather couldn't believe how human it made him look. Maybe Jason had some Homo sapiens DNA in him after all.

"I wouldn't say people gossip at Doctors Circle. They just take a friendly interest in their coworkers," Heather said with more than a trace of irony.

"How much of an interest?"

"They want to know every move you make and every word you say."

"Then I'll be careful how I move and what I say." Jason straightened. For a moment, Heather thought he was going to move aside, until he planted himself even more firmly in her doorway. She glared.

"Is there a problem?" he asked.

Good heavens, was the man trying to be playful? She wasn't in a playful mood.

"Nothing a well-placed kick to the solar plexus wouldn't solve," she said.

"Are you hinting that I'm in the way?" A sparkle flashed deep in those ice-green eyes. He was definitely joking with her. That, or he'd perfected the art of being a royal pain.

"It's more than a hint. Put it in gear, please," Heather said.

"I'll be happy to move if you'll answer one or two questions about that past you claim we don't have," Jason murmured.

"You didn't have any questions the next morning." Heather hoped no one overheard this conversation. She couldn't even imagine the speculation it might provoke.

"I told you…"

"You had a headache," she finished for him. "Correction. You *were* a headache."

"I might have been a touch abrupt," Jason admitted.

She refused to give him the satisfaction of letting him know how much his coldness had bothered her. "That was nearly a year and a half ago. I scarcely remember what you said." Mischievously, she added, "Or what you did, either."

"You concede that I did something?" He appeared torn between curiosity and something that, in an actual full-blooded human, might have been described as vulnerability.

"I concede no such thing," she told him. "As I've mentioned several times, you fell asleep. Don't ask me if you snored. I didn't stick around."

"I passed out," Jason said ruefully. "Jet lag and a couple of drinks will do that to you."

"Not to me," Heather answered. "Well, if you don't remember what happened, why don't you accept my version of it?"

"You haven't given me a version." Up close, the man was taller than she remembered, most likely because she herself barely cleared five foot two.

"I told you, nothing happened. That's as much of a version as I can muster."

"Then why did I find your earring in my bed?" Jason demanded.

Behind him, someone cleared her throat. Heather's blood ran cold. She felt like a kid caught with her hand in a cookie jar.

Jason must have had the same reaction, because he paled. Against his black hair, the high cheekbones and classic jawline stood out in stark relief.

"Dr. Rourke?" came the voice of Cynthia Hernandez, her nurse. "There's a patient waiting in Room C."

"I won't delay you." Jason shifted backward, careful not to bump the dark-haired nurse behind him. That wasn't easy, since Cynthia, six months pregnant with twins, nearly filled the hallway. "See you at four o'clock at my office."

"I'll be there." Heather took the patient's chart from Cynthia and read the cover page. As soon as Jason was gone, she said, "What did you overhear?"

"Nothing, and I wouldn't repeat it if I had." The nurse strolled with her down the hall. "If your earring ended up in Dr. Carmichael's bed, I'm sure it was perfectly innocent."

"Yes, it was." Heather hoped Cynthia was as good as her word. She'd always been trustworthy until now.

Heather also spared a moment to wonder how long Jason would go on refusing to take her word for what had—or rather, hadn't—happened. She hoped she wasn't going to have to tell him the whole truth. After the way he'd behaved the next morning, he didn't deserve to know.

Now that they were colleagues, they'd soon put it all behind them, she figured. It hadn't been such a big deal. Doctors always let their hair down at medical conventions. They didn't always take their clothes off, of course....

She entered the examining room and smiled at the woman sitting on the examining table. Rita Beltran beamed back. Pregnant with triplets after two years of infertility treatments, she'd been floating on a cloud for months.

Heather shoved Jason Carmichael out of her mind. Her heart belonged to her patients, and success stories like Rita's made all her efforts worthwhile.

FROM HIS TEMPORARY, second-story office in the Obstetrics and Gynecology Department, Jason stared across the courtyard. Even in late February, people lingered at the small tables around a fountain. For this time of year, the Southern California weather was remarkably pleasant compared to what he'd grown up with in Boston.

The courtyard connected a trio of buildings: the three-story Birthing Center to the north, plus two curving Spanish-style wings, including the West Wing where he stood. At the plaza level, a couple of workmen were carting boxes into the facing East Wing. He assumed the cartons contained acoustical tiles, since that's what the men had been installing yesterday when the center's administrator, Dr. Patrick Barr, had shown Jason around.

His own clinic. Even stripped to raw flooring and taped windows, it had been gorgeous.

Although he'd loved his work in Virginia, Jason knew he'd made the right decision by coming here. At the larger, better-established facilities where he'd trained and done research in reproductive endocrinology, he'd earned a name for himself. Although he'd enjoyed the prestige, what he loved most was helping eager couples have children.

Established by Dr. Barr's late father, Doctors Circle had significantly improved infant and maternal health in the community. Now it was about to move on to the cutting edge of infertility treatments. Jason treasured the opportunity to put his signature on this new clinic.

Heather Rourke's presence had had nothing to do with his decision to accept the job. Nor had it discouraged him from taking it, either. She had an excellent reputation and they should work well together, as long as she was willing to accept Jason's leadership.

He intended to keep their relationship strictly professional in spite of that irrepressible spark in Heather's eyes. In spite of a feminine way of moving that even a white coat couldn't disguise. In spite of a figure that, while petite in the right places, was also lusciously rounded in others.

In the past, Jason's experiences with romance had ended in unhappiness and anger. That kind of turmoil threatened to interfere with work, which was and always would be his number-one priority. Some men might be cut out for marriage and children, but not him.

A tap at the door drew his attention. George Farajian, chief of the Ob/Gyn Department, poked his graying head into the room. "Okay to come in?"

"Of course." Jason turned away from the window.

"I can't believe how organized you've got the place already." The obstetrician indicated the neatly labeled file cabinets and alphabetized shelves of books.

With a twinge, Jason recalled how he'd chewed out his secretary for unpacking his boxes. If she hadn't, however, he'd have spent the next month or so stumbling over them and cursing because he couldn't find whatever he was looking for. He supposed he owed the woman an apology.

"I have to credit Coral," he said. "She's done a good job."

"Glad to hear it. I believe she was hired specifically with you in mind. Now I'd like to introduce you to your new nurse." George stepped to one side. "Jason, may I present Edith Krick."

The center of gravity in the room shifted as the woman entered. Not literally, although she was heavyset, but emotionally. Dark-skinned, possessed of an inner certitude that bespoke years of experience, Edith had a knowing gaze that swept him assessingly.

They exchanged greetings and shook hands. All the while, Jason felt himself to be under critical scrutiny.

"Edith's one of our best nurses," George said. "She requested this assignment."

"I wanted to work in the Infertility Clinic because I had one baby and never could have any more," Edith told him. "I like to see women have as many as they want. It gets the love to flowing. You can't ever have too much love in this world." From her tone, it sounded as if she were challenging him to disagree.

"Heaven forbid I should stem the flow of love," Jason said drily.

"I expect I'll work real well with your secretary," Edith went on. "Sometimes when a staffer is new in a place, she needs extra encouragement."

So that was the problem. Obviously, Edith had heard about or witnessed Coral's tears and didn't intend to let Jason escape unscathed. Was this entire medical center full of hard-nosed women, he wondered, or was it just his luck to run into two of them on the same day?

George glanced from him to Edith and back again. Clearly, he hadn't missed the undercurrents. "Is everything okay?"

"No problem," Jason said.

"If you don't mind, then, I've got some calls to return. Let me know if you need anything." With a friendly nod, George departed.

"You play golf?" Edith asked.

"Occasionally." Although the change of subject surprised him, Jason tried not to show it. "Do you?"

"No, but Dr. Farajian does. Plays every chance he gets," said the nurse. "Sometimes with Dr. Sentinel. He's our younger obstetrician."

"How about you? How long have you worked at Doctors Circle?" Although Jason didn't want to sound as if he were conducting an interview, it seemed important to take control and shift the balance of gravity back in his own direction.

"Ten years." Apparently, Edith wasn't interested in talking about herself, because she went on to say, "I suppose you know you've got patients scheduled starting on Monday."

"That's right." Although the clinic might not be officially open, Jason wanted to begin screening patients and setting up treatment plans.

"One of them is Loretta Arista," Edith went on. "She's the public relations director here, and if she doesn't get pregnant soon, she's going to give up on having babies altogether."

"I presume Dr. Rourke already did a workup on her?"

"She's tried everything she knows," Edith said. "Now it's your turn."

"I'll do my best." Jason found himself smiling at the woman's obvious concern for her patients. Being a mother hen was a useful quality in a nurse. Less so in a doctor, however. He'd learned the hard way to keep a tight rein on his objectivity.

"We sure will." Edith gave a nod, as if he'd passed inspection. "I'll be honest with you, Doctor. People say you're difficult to work with."

"I set high standards and I'm impatient if they aren't met," Jason told her. "When it comes to infertility, time is the enemy. That's why I hate wasting it. Sloppiness, making assumptions and failing to follow directions won't be tolerated. I'm sure you agree or Dr. Farajian wouldn't have recommended you."

Edith's grin made her face shine. "You're tough because you fight for your patients. I like that."

"I can see that we're going to get along." Jason remembered Heather's comment that Edith had a thick hide. Good. He didn't want to worry about accidentally wounding her ego if he snapped at her under pressure. Most likely, she'd bark right back at him the moment they were alone. Fair enough.

An almost subliminal scent tantalized Jason's nostrils. Heather must have arrived for her tour of the new clinic. His subconscious made the connection even before he saw her.

"Hello, Dr. Rourke. How's everything going with you?" Edith asked the smaller woman hovering outside in the hall.

"Fine. It's good to see you." Briskly, Heather came inside.

An auburn curl straggling along one cheek was the only sign of weariness despite what must have been a long day. Having shed her white coat, she wore a dark skirt and a tailored beige blouse that, in spite of some discreet tucks, sketched her generous curves.

Jason tore his gaze away. He had the uncomfortable sense that both women had noticed where he was looking.

"We're going to check out the clinic," he told Edith. "Care to join us?"

Meaningfully, her chocolate eyes fixed on Heather and him in turn. "Like my mother used to say, three's a crowd," said the nurse. "Right now, this office is so small, I can hardly breathe. Guess I'd better go make sure the Records Department has sent over those patients' charts for next week. I know how you hate inefficiency." Fanning herself with one hand, she stepped outside and closed the door behind her.

Heather's cheeks turned an appealing pink. "She's not very subtle, I'm afraid."

"About what?" Faced with potential embarrassment, Jason had learned that the best response was to pretend you didn't get the point.

"Forget it." She brushed a speck of lint off her blouse, seemingly unaware of how the action emphasized the shape beneath the clothing. Jason struggled to keep his breathing regular.

From the moment they'd met, during registration at a convention hotel in Atlanta, he'd felt the same powerful pull toward her. He found it hard to believe that, even jet-lagged and having consumed a couple of drinks, he'd blacked out as quickly as Heather claimed. Not with such a powerful yearning coursing through him.

Something had happened that night. Jason felt like an idiot for not being able to remember, but that was no excuse for her keeping him in the dark. Heather's earring hadn't landed in his bed by remote control.

Even though it might take a while to pry out the information, he was determined to get an answer. How he responded once he got it would depend on what he learned.

"I'll buy you a cup of coffee at the kiosk on the way over." Jason opened the door for her. "Unless you've had too much caffeine today."

"There's no such thing in this profession. Now that you mention it, if I don't get some more, I may keel over." Heather was so short, she walked under his outstretched arm and cleared it by an inch.

With hardly any effort, Jason could have drawn her against his chest and buried his face in her hair. Rejecting the image, he decided he needed that coffee even more than she did.

Chapter Two

Heather had avoided the first floor of the East Wing since the remodeling began, due to the noise, the sawdust in the air and the hazards of trying to make her way through construction clutter. With Jason as her guide, however, she found herself fascinated.

The work had progressed much further than she'd realized, transforming the area formerly leased to an outside group of pediatricians. The altered layout of the walls showed Heather a state-of-the-art facility, with examining rooms and surgical suites plus an extensive laboratory where they'd be able to offer in vitro fertilization and the whole alphabet soup of new technologies.

In a few short decades, medicine had surpassed what science fiction had proposed when Heather was in high school. In addition to egg donations and embryo transfers, researchers had developed such exotic procedures as AH, or assisted hatching, in which a small opening was etched in the outer coating of the early embryo to help it implant in the womb.

The pace of research had intensified to the point where Heather spent her free time catching up on medical journals, reading research papers and attending conferences.

No matter what people thought, she was grateful to have Jason on staff with his advanced training and experience.

She was less grateful for the man's overwhelming physical presence, not to mention the impulsive way he picked her up and lifted her over a row of boxes blocking her path. His large hands proved surprisingly gentle on her waist, the thumbs clamping lightly across her rib cage, the fingers nudging the skin below her breasts.

Ripples of desire flowed through her, speeding up Heather's breathing and spurring a sharp, Technicolor memory.

When he caught her nipples in his mouth, heat slammed into her, so intense it was almost painful. Lying on the hotel bed, Heather caressed his thick, black hair with a sense of delicious disbelief. She'd only met this man today. What was she doing? And how many times could they do it again during a three-day convention?

"The director's office is this way." Jason, seemingly unaffected after lifting her, led the way past the examining rooms. "You can pick which of the other offices you'd prefer."

"I'll take one as far from yours as possible." Had she said that aloud? Heather managed a smile. "I'm kidding, of course."

"It's up to you." Surely that was studied indifference on Jason's handsome face, not the real thing, she thought, then wondered why she cared.

They stepped through an anteroom into his future office, which consisted of bare walls, rough wooden flooring and a curtainless window. From against the baseboards, Jason hoisted a couple of sketches washed with pastels.

"Dr. Barr asked what I thought of his commissioning a mural for the hall, a motif that would carry through the examining rooms.'' He handed her the samples. ''Here's what the designer is proposing. What do you think?''

The artist had a clever touch with babies, Heather mused as she examined the drawings. Each sketch showed a lively youngster, its face alight with precocious emotions. Rounded and full of life, the infants nearly leaped off the paper and into her arms. They reminded her of some photographs her friend Amy Ravenna Ladd, Doctors Circle's resident psychologist, had installed in her office.

''From your expression, I gather you like them,'' Jason said.

''They're marvelous.'' Heather held them up, trying to imagine how they might figure into a mural. ''Still, some patients find it painful to be constantly reminded of the babies they can't have.''

''Maybe we should post drawings of ancient fertility symbols,'' he teased.

''I suspect they'd prefer male movie stars,'' she said drily. ''That ought to put them in a fertile mood.'' Although she didn't intend to tell him so, she doubted anyone was going to need pictures of movie stars with Dr. Jason Carmichael around.

''Some of our patients are men,'' he pointed out.

''I'll allow a few photos of beautiful women,'' Heather said, adding, ''In the men's bathroom.''

''Whatever you've been doing until now, I was impressed by the statistics on your success rate,'' Jason said. ''Of course, even if I hadn't read the documents, I could tell just by looking around Doctors Circle. There seem to be a lot of pregnant staff members.''

Heather handed the sketches back to him. ''I don't

deserve all the credit. Some women manage fine by themselves.''

"I noticed that your nurse is pregnant," Jason said. "Isn't she uncomfortable, working so close to her due date?"

"She wants to save as much leave as possible for after the twins are born," Heather admitted. "Since she's a single mom…" She stopped, not wanting to reveal more of Cynthia's situation than necessary.

"I see." Jason frowned. "As the single mother of two infants, she could have a hard time keeping up with your schedule. Perhaps she and the father will prefer that she switch to a less rigorous schedule."

"The father's out of the picture entirely." She pressed her lips together, not wanting to say anything further.

"I'm sorry to hear it, for everyone's sake." He shook his head. "She's going to be exhausted and distracted. If she starts making mistakes that affect patient care, she'll have to be transferred."

"She'll be fine." Heather wasn't sure why she bristled at his tone, since she shared the same concerns. But after providing excellent assistance for several years, Cynthia had earned her loyalty. "She loves working with me. She doesn't want any other position."

"Then she should have thought things out more carefully in advance," Jason said.

How dare he blame the pregnancy on Cynthia when she already had enough problems? "Are you blaming her for having an accident?"

"No, but…" Jason seemed briefly at a loss for words. Finally, he said, "As an obstetrical nurse, she surely has the knowledge to prevent this kind of situation."

"People have been known to get carried away by their

passions," Heather said. "Not that I need to mention any names."

She saw by the way his eyes widened that she'd hit her target. "You're changing your story? It's no longer that nothing happened. Now it's that we got carried away by our impulses?"

"We went part of the way before you fell asleep," Heather said. "That's all."

"I'm willing to believe that in my less-than-optimal condition, my memory lost what must have been a delicious experience." Jason moved closer, looming over her. Heather had to fight the impulse to take a step backward. "But you're saying that I fell asleep in the middle of making love to you? That's going a bit far. I'm thirty-six, not ninety-six."

"What difference does it make?" she snapped. "Whatever we did, it's over."

"I'd like to know where I stand."

"A little too close for comfort, frankly."

Deliberately, he shifted toward her. "Let me know when you're ready to run screaming into the woods."

"I should warn you, I know karate." *And several other Japanese words.*

"That won't do any good. The highest you could kick would be my kneecap." He grinned. "You know, the two of us really should spend more time together. Maybe my memories will flood back."

"My memory doesn't need refreshing." Heather had to tilt her head to meet his gaze. "Anything you want to know, you're free to ask. But since you made it clear the next morning that you had no interest in pursuing the matter, I'm surprised you keep harping on it now."

Jason reached out and brushed an errant curl off her temple. His touch shivered straight into parts of Heather that she considered off-limits to him or anybody else. "In my hungover condition, I may have muttered something less than gallant. For that, I apologize."

"Your exact words, as I recall, were, 'Whatever happened last night, I trust I'll hear nothing further about it.'" A slight tremor undermined Heather's tone. Darn it, she didn't want to show any vulnerability around Jason.

He had no right to know how much he'd wounded her. For the first time in years, she'd begun to open up to a man, only to have him throw it in her face.

If she'd had different life experiences, she might have found his attitude merely churlish and dismissed it from her mind. To a woman who'd been abandoned as a teenager by the man she'd loved and trusted, however, his rejection had struck her like a physical blow.

"Did I really say that?" Jason asked. "Ouch."

"Those were your exact words. I already explained that there's nothing wrong with my memory." Heather was preparing a few more sharp remarks when she saw him focus on a spot behind her and realized someone had come into the room.

She turned, already knowing there was only one person at Doctors Circle who could approach that quietly on bare floors. Coral Liu possessed an inner calm that had impressed Heather from the moment the young woman started work in January. Even now, when she was probably quaking inside at facing her boss, her smooth, intelligent face showed only respect.

"I hope I'm not interrupting." Coral held up a catalog of office furniture. "Mrs. Barr asked me to show you this. I thought it might be helpful to make your selections while you're in the new office, so you can picture how things would fit."

With an impatient expulsion of breath, Jason took the catalog. "I don't have much of an eye for interior decorating."

Coral bit her lip. Jason's slight sign of impatience bothered her, Heather could tell. It was too bad such a rough-edged man had been paired with a sensitive secretary, although she knew Natalie had interviewed a number of applicants before recommending Coral.

"I took the liberty of drawing a floor plan, if you'd care to look at it," the secretary said.

"Sure." Jason didn't lift his eyes from the catalog as he flipped through.

Coral handed Heather a sheet of paper. Although the markings had been sketched with a tentative hand, the young woman had done a careful job of arranging the desk, a couch, chairs and filing cabinets. "Looks good to me."

Jason gave it a quick glance. "Might work. I'll give it a more thorough going-over later." He handed everything back to Coral. "Put these on my desk, please."

"Yes, Dr. Carmichael." She turned away, disappointment clouding her eyes. Apparently she'd hoped her floor plan would draw a more positive response.

"Oh, Coral. One more thing."

She stopped, her slim back rigid, and turned to face him.

"On second thought, I realize it wasn't such a bad idea to unpack my files and books," Jason said. "We won't be moving for at least a month, and I'd have hated not being able to find things when I needed them. In future, just check with me before doing something like that, okay?"

"Yes, sir." After giving him a shy smile, Coral retreated. Her shoulders, Heather noticed, had relaxed.

"What were we talking about?" Jason asked after Coral had left. "Something important, I recall."

Heather refused to resume the discussion of their ill-starred encounter in Atlanta. "We were reviewing the mural. I approve of it. Babies, babies everywhere sets the right tone."

"I'll tell Patrick. As I said before, decorating isn't my strong point." Despite his well-known dislike of wasting time, Jason appeared in no hurry to move on. "The rest of our new staff should be on board before April. I'll forward their bios to you, if you're interested."

"I'd like that." Time to make her getaway, Heather decided. "Thanks for showing me around. I have to be going."

"You haven't picked your office."

"I'll leave that to you," she said. "I've got an appointment."

Although technically she was finished at five o'clock, infertility patients had to be seen during their optimal times of the month, which weren't always predictable. Some of the women also contended with rigid work schedules, so Heather made a point of staying flexible.

"I'll see you later, then." Jason didn't suggest walking back across the plaza together, to her relief.

Once she was out in the fresh air, Heather's spirits rose. With luck, they had put that entire Atlanta business behind them. With a little more luck, the sensual awareness vibrating between them would abate as soon as familiarity bred boredom. Any day now.

She marched across the courtyard, her sensible pumps clicking confidently against the pavement.

"TELL ME AGAIN what was wrong with this one," Rob Sentinel said as he and Jason emerged from the third apartment building they'd visited.

Jason appreciated the young obstetrician's offer to spend part of Saturday ferrying him around town. As a recent arrival himself, Rob knew the ropes of apartment hunting.

"There was no built-in microwave," Jason said.

"That's what I thought you said. I just didn't believe it. They sell microwaves at discount stores, you know." Rob sounded impatient, which was understandable, considering that he'd given up a chance to play golf with George today.

"I've already accumulated more stuff than I want." Jason knew it didn't make sense, his dislike of loading himself down with material possessions. Still, with only a few clothes, a small TV and a boom box, he'd been able to ship everything easily from Virginia.

If he had good financial sense, he'd buy a place, his mother had advised in a phone call from Boston. Being a real estate agent, she figured he was making a mistake by not investing now that he appeared to be putting down roots.

Certainly Jason didn't plan to change jobs any time soon. Possibly not for many years.

Yet in the past there'd been times—one in particular, after his engagement had fallen apart—when both his personal and professional lives had benefited from his ability to pack up and move on short notice. He wasn't ready to give up that freedom yet.

"Hold on." Rob paused next to his car and folded his arms. "Didn't you ask me earlier whether any of the apartments allowed dogs? A dog isn't exactly what I'd call a minor acquisition."

"It was an idle question." Jason had always dreamed

of having a dog. His parents, who took pride in their spotless Brookline home, had nixed the idea while he was growing up, and he'd had no opportunity since then. "Maybe when I retire, I'll buy a large place and a dog to go with it. I don't know why I bothered asking today. It just popped into my head."

For some reason, he wondered whether Heather liked dogs. He'd spent the last couple of days wondering about Heather's taste in a lot of things, although he'd been too busy to seek her out again.

"Your subconscious might be sending you a signal," said his companion.

"Excuse me?" How on earth had Rob figured out that he was thinking about Heather?

"The dog. If that's what you really want, we're taking the wrong approach." The obstetrician leaned against the car. "I don't think an apartment is what you need."

"If you're about to suggest I invest in real estate, stop right there," Jason said.

"I was thinking more along the lines of renting a house or a town house," the younger doctor said. "That's what Dr. Rourke does."

"Oh?" He tried to sound casual, although he found himself intensely interested in hearing more. "Where does she live?"

"In a town house development on Bordeaux Avenue. That's in the northeastern part of town," Rob said. "I'd have rented there myself if it were closer to the beach."

"Do they allow pets?" That would be ideal, Jason thought.

"I don't know," said the other doctor. "You could ask her about it on Monday."

"I don't want to wait that long. I'm tired of the hotel." He was impatient to get settled and curious to see where Heather lived, too. "Why don't we swing by there and take a look at her place?"

"I don't know her unit number. Besides, she's probably not home." Obviously, Rob wasn't eager to make another stop. If he were getting tired of the apartment hunt, Jason couldn't blame him.

"You've been great today," he said. "You've given me a good idea of what's available. Why don't you drop me at my hotel? I can take it from there."

"I promised to help," Rob said stubbornly. "Besides, you don't know your way around town."

"I've got a map," he pointed out, then added the kicker. "It's still early enough to hit the golf course."

The man ran through several expressions as he waged an internal debate. "All right." The call of the links had won out. "I'll take you back, but let me know if you need more help."

"You bet." Jason didn't plan to do anything of the sort.

At his hotel, he thanked Rob. As soon as the man was out of sight, Jason called Patrick's home. The administrator had given him the number in case of weekend or evening problems that required his immediate attention.

Patrick's wife, Natalie, answered. After Jason explained that he wanted to check out the town houses, she gave him Heather's address and cell phone number. "I'm not sure if she's home," Natalie said. "She volunteers in a program for unwed mothers on Saturday mornings."

Into Jason's mind flashed their conversation on Wednesday about the pregnant nurse, along with Heather's sharp reaction. Had she misinterpreted his remarks as an insult toward unmarried mothers? He'd only meant to point out that, if anyone knew enough to take precautions, it ought to be an obstetrical nurse.

"It's nearly noon," he said. "She might be home."

"You can call her," Natalie said.

"I appreciate the information."

"Good luck on finding a place."

"Thanks." Jason didn't mean to mislead her, but, as he rang off, he'd already decided not to bother calling in advance.

Heather might tell him to stay away. And he had no intention of doing that.

Chapter Three

Pushing up on her hands and knees, the baby rocked her little body forward, lost her balance and plopped onto the carpet. Doggedly, she hoisted herself up again and began rocking once more.

"She's trying to crawl," Heather said in delight.

"Wait! I'll get my camera." Her daughter Olive ran for the digital apparatus, which was never far away. "I have to send John a shot."

"He's getting out of the marines next month," Heather pointed out. "He'll be able to watch her crawl and stand and walk before you know it."

"I can't bear for him to miss any of it. He's miserable that he wasn't here for her birth." Crouching, Olive took aim and snapped a shot just as Ginger flopped onto her side and opened her mouth to bawl. "Oh, no. That's going to look awful."

"It's cute," Heather said. "Everything she does is cute."

"Typical grandmother." Her daughter smiled indulgently. "Even if you are ridiculously young."

"You think she's cute, too!"

"Granted, but I don't dote on her the way you do." With an arch look, Olive added, "Maybe if you could brag about her to your friends, you'd get it out of your system.''

"I do brag about her to my friends."

"Only Natalie and Amy." Olive stretched onto her stomach, keeping the baby in the frame. When it came to taking pictures, she had a lot of patience. "I know you're not ashamed of us, Mom, but you need to get over being ashamed of yourself."

That was perceptive for a twenty-one-year-old woman, Heather reflected. "Things have changed. When I got pregnant out of wedlock, people sneered at me. I was held up as a bad example."

"Oh, come on! Even twenty years ago, nobody believed that old business about fallen women."

"You'd be surprised."

Olive clicked quietly as Ginger tried again. This time, the baby managed to move her arms and legs fast enough to keep her balance as she lurched forward. "She did it!"

"I'm going to get my camera, too," Heather said. "Don't let her grow up before I get back."

She'd scarcely taken two steps before the phone rang in the kitchen. It was John, making one of his rare overseas calls to his fiancée. After they exchanged greetings, she went to get her daughter.

Olive vanished to take the call. In the living room, Heather indulged herself by shooting a series of photos as Ginger bumbled her way along the carpet, making a colorful splash with her yellow jumpsuit and carrot-colored hair.

Although Olive and Ginger had been staying here for five months, she still could hardly believe she'd not only been reunited with her daughter, she'd also gained a granddaughter. It was more than she'd ever dared hope for.

Heather had been a confused fifteen-year-old when she got pregnant by her eighteen-year-old boyfriend, Ned. A handsome young man with a tan complexion and dark hair like Olive's, he'd sworn he adored her and wanted to marry her someday—until he discovered that she was with child.

The first words out of his mouth had been, "It's not mine." Shocked, she'd burst into tears. He was the only man she'd ever been with, she'd pointed out. They loved each other, didn't they? Surely he was going to stand by her.

What a fool she'd been! For the next few weeks, Ned had avoided her. When Heather showed up at the auto repair shop where he worked, he'd ordered her off the premises.

She'd spent a miserable week confiding in no one, telling herself Ned would come to his senses. Finally she'd dropped by his house. His mother had fixed her with an angry glare.

"He's gone," the woman had said. "Don't ask me where. It's your fault. He should never have gotten mixed up with a tramp like you."

Stunned and frightened by the thought of what lay ahead, Heather had cried until her eyes were raw, then gone home and confessed to her parents. Seeing the disappointment in their faces had been almost as bad as experiencing Ned's betrayal.

Her father, a truck driver, and her mother, a supermarket checker, had always encouraged Heather and her brother to focus on their studies and aim for the stars. News of the pregnancy had hit them hard.

They hadn't rejected her, though. Their love had made

life bearable while she attended an alternative high school and suffered snubs from former friends. When the baby was born, Heather had known she wasn't prepared to raise a child, so she'd tearfully given her up for adoption. At every point, her parents had delivered their support without question.

"I'll never let you down again," she'd told them, and she hadn't. When she graduated from college, the first person in her family to do so, they'd been thrilled, and she'd been pleased when her brother followed in her footsteps.

Earning her medical degree, although it required financial sacrifices of everyone, had filled them with pride. So had Heather's brother's decision to become a police officer.

Over the years, she'd always wondered where her little girl was and hoped she was loved. Although Heather had never doubted the wisdom of her decision, she'd ached for the child she would never see.

A few years ago, she'd signed up with a service that matched parents and birth children, in case her daughter ever wanted to find her. About a year ago, she'd received a call.

Olive's beloved adoptive parents had died in an accident while she was in college. Engaged to a marine, pregnant and temporarily alone while he served overseas, she'd sought to connect with the woman who'd given birth to her.

As soon as they met, they'd become best friends. From her flashing brown eyes to her sense of humor, Olive seemed like a younger sister. Even the parts of her that came from Ned, like her dark hair and slim build, were a gift, in Heather's opinion. The man was a fool who'd lost much more than he'd taken.

She could never regret having this daughter and granddaughter, no matter how much they'd cost her. And she knew her parents, who'd met them at Christmas, no longer regretted it, either.

There'd been plenty of speculation at Doctors Circle last fall when Heather, without explanation, took two months leave to coach Olive through the birth and spend time with her afterward. Office gossip attributed her absence to pique at Jason's appointment, and she'd done nothing to correct the impression. It made as good an excuse as any, since she had no intention of subjecting her painful past to the scrutiny of others.

Afterward, the pair had come to live here while John wrapped up his service. Olive, who'd grown up only an hour's drive away in Los Angeles, had finished earning her degree at nearby Serene College. This month, she'd taken her last final and completed her work. Soon, John would be returning.

Heather didn't want to think about how much she was going to miss living with her daughter and granddaughter. Strange as it seemed, she enjoyed having her once-tranquil living room crammed with a playpen and toys and she loved being called Mom, an honor Olive had spontaneously bestowed upon her. She hoped the new family would settle nearby so she could watch every step, literally and figuratively, of Ginger's development.

"Mom!" Olive sprinted into the living room. "I'm so excited! John wants to get married as soon as he arrives. He can't bear to wait, and neither can I! We're going to have our wedding next month."

"I'm pleased for you." Relief was Heather's first reaction. She'd never met her future son-in-law in person, and until now had had only Olive's assurances that he was loving and rock-solid. Thank goodness John hadn't turned out to be a cad like Ned.

"It's been so lonely with him gone, and now we'll be together all the time." Joy made Olive shimmer as she sang, "Here comes the bride! Big, fat and wide! Not!"

Despite Heather's happiness for her daughter, reality intruded. A little less than three weeks. That was all the time they had until John returned.

"How will we ever be able to put a wedding together?" she cried. "Oh, honey, I'm sorry. I don't mean to be a spoilsport and I know Amy managed hers in a week, but I have no idea where to begin."

Amy and Quent Ladd had married quickly in order to gain custody of his orphaned niece and nephew. They'd been assisted by Amy's highly capable Aunt Mary, who'd offered the use of her large home for the ceremony and reception. This town home, despite its vaulted ceiling and graceful design, wasn't nearly big enough, in Heather's opinion.

"You're such a worrier," chortled her daughter. "We're going to get married at a Las Vegas wedding chapel. The only guests will be you and John's parents from Texas. You'll bring the baby home and watch her for me during our honeymoon, won't you? We're going to celebrate right there in Vegas."

"Of course," Heather said.

Olive performed an impromptu dance that made Ginger laugh. "Your daddy's coming home! I'm going to be a bride!"

"You need a dress," Heather said.

"John told me to pick out a ring, too." Olive started for the kitchen again.

"Where are you going?"

"To call my friend Julia to help me shop. I know how

impatient you get in stores," her daughter said. "Don't argue. I'll let you see what I choose before I make the final decision, okay?"

"All right." Despite her sense that the mother of the bride ought to have a finger in every pie, Heather knew that after one hour in the mall, she'd start tapping her foot and biting her nails. "Leave the baby with me while you shop."

"Julia would have a fit. She's always complaining that she doesn't get to spend enough time with Ginger."

"Babies don't make good shopping companions. She'll get restless," Heather warned.

"We'll take lots of breaks," Olive said. "Don't fuss over me, Mom. Not that I really mind. Gosh, you're so much like my mama used to be, I almost feel like she's here."

"I'm sure she is." Heather felt a deep gratitude to the woman who'd raised Olive. "She'll always be here in your heart."

Her daughter's eyes got suspiciously bright. She hurried to stuff supplies into the diaper bag. By the time she whisked Ginger out the door, Olive was dry-eyed and eager to look for a gown.

After the door closed, the two most precious people in Heather's life were gone, if only for a little while. The sparkle vanished from the air.

"So this is what empty-nest syndrome feels like," she told the silent house. "It's not as if I'd spent twenty years being a mother. I shouldn't make such a big deal of it."

With a sigh, she bent to pick up the scattered toys that had accumulated on the carpet along with bits of lint and shreds of paper. They must be transporting themselves

here from an alternate universe, because Heather had
never figured out where all this stuff came from.

The doorbell rang. Olive had forgotten something,
which wasn't surprising in view of her rush. Pushing a
flyaway strand of hair from her forehead, Heather went
to answer the door.

The dark-haired man who filled the doorway regarded
her with amused curiosity. "Just getting up, at this
hour?" he asked.

Uncomfortably, Heather realized what a picture she
must make. After rising early to feed Ginger while Olive
slept, she'd showered and thrown on a sweatsuit that
resembled pajamas. Although she'd brushed her hair,
that was many hours and diaper changes ago.

Jason, by contrast, looked as if he'd strolled out of a
magazine ad. It was positively indecent the way his polo
shirt stretched across his broad chest and his jeans hung
low across his hips. It looked as if one tweak would be
enough to make the snap give way.

Stop thinking like that! "I'm getting a head start on
my spring cleaning," Heather improvised. "What can I
do for you?"

"I'm house-hunting and got curious about where you
lived." With a swift motion, he plucked a wisp of paper
from her hair. "Did you hold a confetti parade through
your premises this morning?" He peered past her into
the entryway.

With a jolt, Heather realized that if she opened the
door any further, he'd see the playpen in the living room
and the high chair visible through the doorway in the
kitchen. Not to mention assorted toys and parenting
magazines.

"Yes, I had a parade, and that's why you can't come
in," she said tartly. "There's horse poop everywhere."

Jason's smile turned into a grimace. "That's the weirdest excuse I've ever heard."

"For what?"

"For keeping me out."

"Women make a lot of excuses for keeping you out, do they?" Heather said. "The truth is, as you can see, I'm in no shape to receive company."

He composed his features into a semblance of injured innocence. "I'm simply looking for ideas about what kind of place to rent."

"That's easy. Don't rent, buy," Heather said. "That's what I'm going to do as soon as I save the down payment." If she hadn't been repaying student loans until the previous year, she'd have purchased a house long ago.

"If you're planning to close the door on my foot, it won't work," Jason said. "I'm wearing heavy shoes."

"Why would I need to close the door on your foot, since you're going away?"

He edged closer. "I just want to take a look at the layout of your town house. I've been thinking of renting here in the development."

Dismay squeezed the air from Heather's lungs. Jason, living in her complex? That would mean running into each other at the mailboxes and the pool. He'd see her in her bikini. What was worse, he'd see Olive and Ginger.

"You'd hate it," she said. "It's noisy."

"It seems quiet today." Sure enough, the only sounds were birds twittering in a tree and the hum of a car passing on the street. "I'm sure it'll be fine."

Dropping the noise angle, Heather shifted to a more promising topic. "You should check out the area where

Amy and Quent Ladd live, near the beach. It's much more suitable for a single person.''

"Why don't you live there?" he asked.

"Because I'm stuffy and conventional." This wasn't working, she could tell by his stubborn stance. "I'll tell you what. Wait out there while I change, and I'll take you to meet the manager. I'm sure she'd be happy to…"

He'd leaned a bit too far toward her. Even a strong guy like Jason could only challenge gravity so far before he lost his balance, and at the merest bump from his strong shoulder, Heather staggered backward. The door swung wider.

"I'm sorry." Jason grabbed her arm in time to prevent a tumble. "I'm not usually this clumsy." His head came up as he took in the contents of the room. There was a long, contemplative pause. "When did you start running a day-care center?"

"Believe it or not, one baby created all this mess. My niece and her daughter are visiting." Heather hated to lie, but if there was anyone she didn't choose to bare her soul to, it was Jason Carmichael. Especially after that comment about how Cynthia should have known better than to get pregnant out of wedlock.

"Great architecture." Apparently accepting her explanation, he indicated the high ceiling and open staircase. "How's the construction?"

On the verge of praising it, she remembered her goal of discouraging him from renting in the complex. "The upstairs bathroom tilts. There are cracks in the walls, too." That was true, more or less. Practically every wall in Southern California had a few cosmetic cracks, thanks to the occasional earthquakes.

"There's got to be some reason you chose to live here," he said.

Darn the man, why did he insist on questioning her so closely? He took far too great an interest in Heather's home for her comfort.

"I'll show you," she said, deciding openness was the only way to satisfy his curiosity. "Follow me."

She led him through the living room. The angles and sightlines felt different when she tried to regard them from Jason's point of view. Or perhaps it was his thoroughly male, keenly inquisitive presence that changed everything.

He radiated a subtle energy, a vibration that filled the town house. Heather battled the instinct to touch him. In spite of herself, she knew where that could lead and wasn't absolutely certain she'd be able to stop.

In the kitchen, Jason's eyebrows rose at the sight of the high chair. "Your niece brought a lot of equipment for a visit."

"She's staying with me while she finishes college," Heather clarified. On the point of mentioning that Olive was getting married next month, she stopped. Guilty people gave themselves away by prattling too much, and the more she talked, the more suspicious he was likely to become.

"You're a gracious aunt to put up with all this mess," he said.

Heather's gaze traveled across the unwashed dishes on the counter to a bib smeared with breakfast food. She supposed it was disorderly from the point of view of a man who had only himself to care for. Until this moment, she'd hardly noticed. "I don't mind. It's only temporary."

"At least the kitchen is a good size," he said approvingly.

Heather tried to find some flaw to point out, but failed.

Reaching the glass door, she slid it open and stepped onto the enclosed patio. "This is the reason I rented the place." She indicated a small flowerbed bursting with cool-weather flowers suitable for a Southern California winter.

"It's very pretty. You like to garden?" Jason asked.

"I'd love to have a whole yard full of flowers." Heather's mind painted the scene as she spoke. "Rose bushes in every corner and climbing on a trellis. I want enough blooms for cutting and the air filled with old-fashioned perfume."

"You've got it planned out, I see." Jason edged away, or perhaps he was turning to examine a potted coleus. "I can't imagine where you find the time."

"Gardening's restful," Heather said. "Digging in the dirt settles my mind."

His teasing manner of a few minutes ago disappeared. "It looks to me like a lot of effort for a place you're going to leave behind eventually." Heather could have sworn she saw disapproval in the way he regarded the rioting flowerbed.

"Sticking a few bedding plants into the ground isn't exactly a lifetime commitment," she said. "Besides, these are annual flowers. They have to be replaced a couple of times a year in any case."

"Suit yourself," Jason said.

She couldn't resist teasing him. "If you decide to lease a unit, I'll be glad to offer you tips. You might become a real aficionado."

"I can't imagine investing that much effort in something I'm going to leave behind," Jason answered. "It's a waste of effort."

"How soon are you planning to move on?" Heather leaned down and yanked a weed.

In the midday light, Jason's green eyes took on a hard emerald gloss. "Not soon, of course, but let's be honest. Although heading this clinic is a terrific opportunity, I don't picture myself sticking around forever."

"No roses and no roots," Heather said. "How sad."

Jason shrugged. "A house is just a place."

She imagined him as an old man, living in Spartan quarters, still refusing to commit himself to anything beyond his profession. Feeling a pinch of regret, she conceded silently that, without meaning to, she'd begun to picture Jason in a romantic light. The man was so darn handsome, and the way he moved sent shivers down her spine.

She ought to know better. Thank goodness he'd brought her up short today. There were good men in the world, such as her friends' husbands, but they were few and far between. Too many were like Ned, quick to promise the moon and ready to run when a woman needed them.

Or like Jason, who valued only the professional side of himself. There was no point in arguing with him. The man was as set in his ways as concrete.

After dusting off her hands, Heather took him back inside. "I'd show you the bedrooms but they're in worse shape than the kitchen."

A subdued Jason didn't press the point. "Thanks for the tour. I'll see you at work on Monday."

"Good luck finding a place to live." Although it might be unwise, she found herself adding, "Did you decide against renting a town house?"

"It's a bit large for a single guy. I wouldn't want to inadvertently encourage any relatives to move in with me, particularly ones with babies," he said, and let himself out.

Maybe he was joking, but Heather didn't find the remark funny. She was tempted to throw one of Ginger's
toys at his retreating back.

She couldn't imagine why she'd ever allowed herself
to be attracted to that stuffed shirt. Okay, Jason could
be charming when he turned the frost level down to low,
but with him, as with most men she'd met, you never
knew when you were going to get a blast of arctic air
in the face.

Well, Heather had better things to do with her Saturday than stand here hurling mental insults at Jason
Carmichael. Even a woman with a limited attention span
for mall shopping could help her daughter get married.

She switched on her computer, logged on to the Internet and cruised the wedding-related websites, book-
marking pages with gowns she thought Olive might like.
Being the mother of the bride provided a lot more satisfaction than she'd ever found or ever expected to find
with a man.

Chapter Four

The three puppies wiggled in their basket, barking excitedly and trying to pour over the edges. Two little boys whom Jason guessed to be about six and eight kept stuffing them back inside.

"Hi, there." He crouched on the walkway and scratched each set of floppy ears in turn. Eager pink tongues swiped his hand and one pup, a shaggy black-and-tan shepherd mix, leaped as if trying to land in his lap.

"You want one, mister? They're ten dollars." The older boy pointed at a hand-lettered sign for confirmation. "Our mom says we can't keep them."

"Neither can I, I'm afraid." After spending Saturday and most of today exhausting rental possibilities, Jason had returned to Heather's development in earnest a short time earlier. Yesterday, he'd been so put off by the notion of nesting that he'd ignored a sign at the manager's office advertising a unit for rent. He hadn't forgotten about it, though.

By comparison to everything else he'd seen, he'd found the empty town house to his liking. Located halfway across the complex from Heather's, it featured a similar layout and came furnished. The only vegetation

on its patio was a ficus tree watered through an auto-
matic system.

Jason had signed up immediately. The month-to-
month lease meant that if he found something he liked
better, he was free to move. Because of the location,
there was no reason for him and Heather to get in each
other's way, and he appreciated the peace and quiet.

The one drawback was that renters weren't allowed
to have pets. The manager had explained that owner-
occupants could keep animals as long as they didn't allow them to run loose. The boys' family must be owners,
Jason thought.

"That's Frodo. He's my favorite." The younger boy
indicated the black-and-tan pup, whose tail was wagging
so hard that Jason half expected it to propel its owner
into the air.

"I can't have a dog because I'm renting," he said.

The older boy's face scrunched. "What's the use of
being a grown-up if you can't have a dog?"

"Good point." Jason got to his feet. "I hope you find
homes for them."

"Thanks," they chorused.

What *was* the use of being a grown-up if you couldn't
have a puppy or roses or any other reasonable thing that
you wanted? he mused. It was an internal discussion that
would have surprised Heather Rourke, Jason supposed.

He'd certainly bristled when she'd showed him her
flower garden. Its blooming lushness had filled his
senses with perfume and his soul with an intense yearning. For what, he wasn't sure, but he'd yanked himself
back to reality in a big hurry.

As he strolled around the complex to check out its
amenities, Jason wondered if he would ever feel ready
to settle down in one place or with one woman. He

didn't believe in love sweeping people off their feet, though, especially not a scientist like him. Some guys weren't cut out to be husbands, and he was one of them.

He tried to remember what impulse had prompted him to get engaged during his residency. He'd met Eileen, a law student at Boston University, through family friends. They'd had a lot in common, including busy schedules, a taste for Greek food and a love of jazz. Eileen had understood about Jason's long hours and seemed to share his vision of a future devoted to becoming among the best in their fields.

Somewhere along the line, the subject of marriage had come up. Knowing that he needed a wife with similar goals and attitudes, Jason had fallen in with the idea. Both of them agreed that they wanted to work the long hours required by their professions, with children postponed indefinitely.

He tensed as he recalled his last year of residency. During a difficult period, he'd driven himself harder and, he knew, become snappish to those around him. Perversely, Eileen had chosen that time to press him to set a date for their wedding.

He'd told her frankly that he couldn't handle getting married right then and needed the freedom to relocate if necessary. Her response had been tears and nagging. Jason knew he should have tried to understand, but he hadn't possessed the energy to deal with her. When a prominent institution in England invited him to pursue his work there after completing his residency, he'd ended his engagement and removed himself from the situation.

Later, through friends, he'd learned that Eileen had planned to drop out of law school and didn't want a demanding career. She wasn't crazy about Greek food or jazz, either. Their relationship had been built on her molding herself to suit him, without his realizing it. Perhaps she hadn't been honest with herself about what she was doing, either.

Although Jason regretted having disappointed her, marriage would have been a huge mistake. Perhaps that was why he'd reacted so strongly to the flowers yesterday. Subconsciously, he'd pegged Heather as being dedicated to her work, and it disturbed him to discover that at heart what she wanted was the whole picket-fence, rose-trellis scenario. Just like Eileen.

Seeing the playpen and toys in her living room had given him a start, too. Oddly, Jason had found them kind of appealing, although he was relieved to know they belonged to Heather's niece.

Babies were cute. So were little boys like the pair with the puppies. Their dad probably loved taking them to ball games and playing on the beach with them. Someday, Jason supposed, he might want kids of his own. Someday, like in another ten years.

Lost in thought, he didn't realize he was passing Heather's unit until he saw her standing in front, trimming dead blossoms from an azalea. In a tan T-shirt and beige jeans, she was shapely enough to catch any man's eye.

When she caught sight of Jason, her hand jerked and she mangled a branch. "What are you doing here?"

"I'm glad to see you, too," he said.

Heather ducked her head, acknowledging the veiled complaint. "You're right. It's nice to see you again, Dr. Carmichael. Did you have some questions about the care and feeding of rose bushes?"

"I'm afraid not," he said. "If you see me traipsing

by later with my arms full, you can lend a hand if you care to."

Her half smile shaded into a frown. "You rented a place?"

He shrugged. "Serene Beach turns out not to have a very big supply of available housing."

"You swore you'd decided against renting a town house."

"That was before I looked all over town," Jason said. "I honestly tried to find a place somewhere else. I combed the newspaper and an Internet referral service."

"You haven't been looking very long," Heather retorted mercilessly.

"I'm sick of the hotel and I've got a busy week ahead." He knew it was a low blow, to use work as an excuse for encroaching on her territory, but it truly was part of the reason for his rush. "There's no reason for us to see each other except in passing."

"We'll run into each other at the pool," she countered.

The image that came to mind, of Heather's full breasts and slim waist displayed in a bikini, almost broke down Jason's determination to regard her purely as a colleague. His voice catching, he choked out, "I don't plan to do much swimming."

"Good." Returning her attention to the azalea, she cut the broken branch and tossed it into a plastic bucket. "I trust you won't be running over to borrow a cup of sugar or a pair of pruning shears."

"Scout's honor." She hadn't mentioned laundry detergent, he thought. He might run out of that.

"And don't you dare go anywhere near my health club!"

"Which health club is that?" he asked, his interest perking.

"Never mind." Heather appeared fascinated by a weed near the base of the bush. "I'll see you around."

"You bet." Although he would have enjoyed lingering, Jason knew he had a lot to accomplish this evening.

With a wave, he strode away, his thoughts flying ahead to the process of moving. The heated buzz in his nervous system abated too slowly for comfort.

A health club, eh? He'd make a point of finding it. A man needed exercise, after all.

"OH, COME ON, Mom," Olive said. "You can't tell me his moving here doesn't mean he likes you. I can't wait to meet this guy!"

"Jason Carmichael is my boss and an annoying one, at that." Heather glowered. The last thing she wanted was for her daughter to start trying to pair them off.

"That doesn't mean he can't be interested in you! Besides, he's your supervisor, not your boss. He doesn't have the power to fire you, does he?"

"No." The hospital administrator was the only one who had that right.

"See?" Olive crowed.

"He needs a place to live. That's all." Heather clicked to another page on the computer screen. "What do you think of this one? I wasn't sure whether you liked scooped necklines."

"So I can show off my nonexistent cleavage?" Her daughter sighed. "I wish I'd inherited your figure, Mom."

"You have a great figure!"

"Not as great as yours."

"I have a hard time finding clothes that don't make me look fat," Heather protested.

"What you look is stacked," Olive said. "No wonder this hunky guy wants to be our neighbor."

When Heather had mentioned Jason's first visit the previous day, Olive had been too distracted by her armful of brochures and brainful of wedding ideas to pay much attention. After learning that he'd actually rented a place, however, she'd seized on the topic with glee.

"You've never met him," Heather pointed out. "What makes you think he's hunky?"

"The little smile you wear every time you mention him." Leaning over her, Olive flicked from one web page to another so rapidly that Heather couldn't keep track of what they were looking at. She supposed you had to be under twenty-five to master that skill. "You smile the same way whenever you see one of your favorite actors."

"Oh, seriously!" she scoffed.

Olive paused at a Victorian-style gown, studied it intently for about five seconds, then zoomed onward. "Let me guess. He's tall, dark and handsome."

Heather wondered if her daughter were psychic, since her taste in movie stars was wide-ranging. "How on earth did you know that?"

"Because my father must have been." Olive paused in her surfing. "Obviously I didn't get my coloring from you."

"You have my eyes, though. Ned's were darker." Heather smiled. "It's funny how the red hair skipped a generation."

"You haven't met John yet," Olive pointed out.

In Olive's favorite photo, they both wore ski caps and

jackets. Until now, Heather hadn't realized she'd never seen his hair.

"He has red hair?"

"Like a carrot with a sunburn."

Olive logged off the Internet. She must be nearing wedding overload, at least for the moment. Besides, it was dinnertime.

The younger woman set the table while Heather made spaghetti. "You should invite him for dinner," Olive said as she worked.

"By 'him,' should I assume you mean Jason?" Heather checked the hot water, but it wasn't quite at a boil yet.

"None other." Olive clinked down two plates.

"I'd be happy if I never saw him outside the office again." She meant it. Brisk professionalism was the best attitude to adopt where that man was concerned.

"What's his voice like?" Olive turned to offer Ginger another spoonful of baby food. Strapped into her high chair, the little girl swallowed it hungrily.

"What difference does it make?"

"There's nothing like a sexy voice." Olive paused as if listening to something Heather couldn't hear. "John has a slow, sensuous way of talking. I guess it's the Texas accent. What kind of accent does Jason have?"

"Boston." Heather hadn't given it any thought until now. "Not a strong one, though." And a deep voice, but she wasn't going to give her daughter the satisfaction of mentioning it.

"Mom, have you had a serious relationship in your entire life?" Olive resumed feeding Ginger. "I mean, aside from my father?"

After their reunion, Heather had related the story of their ill-starred romance, softened to depict Ned as immature rather than self-centered. To Heather's relief, her daughter had shown no interest in locating him.

"No. I haven't met a man I could love. Sometimes I doubt he exists." Although Heather dated from time to time, her self-protective instincts had led her to keep men at bay, at least until that night with Jason. In retrospect, she was grateful that he'd fallen asleep. If they'd made love, his thoughtless remark the next morning would have been devastating.

"Stop!" Olive waved excitedly.

Looking down, Heather discovered she'd been about to drop the uncooked spaghetti into the simmering tomato sauce instead of the boiling water. "Oops. Thanks for warning me."

"Don't try to convince me you weren't daydreaming about someone of the male persuasion." Her daughter grinned. "Care to mention any names?"

"Brad Pitt," Heather said quickly. "Ewan McGregor. Heath Ledger."

"Jason Carmichael?" suggested her impish tormentor.

"Why does he fascinate you so much?" Heather stirred the spaghetti with a pasta fork, separating the strands.

"It's long past time you got over my father being such a jerk." Apparently Olive had drawn her own conclusions about Ned's behavior despite Heather's attempt to spare her the worst. "Maybe it's because John and I are so happy that I want you to find the right man, too."

"I have no problem with that," said Heather. "When I find him, I'll let you know."

"Sure you will." Skepticism rang in every word.

Heather hoped this was the last she'd hear of the topic. She didn't need a matchmaker living in the same house,

particularly one who'd seized on the misguided notion
that there was some kind of chemistry between her and
Jason.

With luck, plans for the wedding would put the whole
thing out of Olive's mind soon enough, she told herself,
and switched off the burner under the tomato sauce.

THE PATIENT was thirty-four years old and had been trying to get pregnant for five years. She and her husband
had undergone a battery of tests with no definitive explanation for their infertility, which was often the case
despite advances in medicine.

Loretta Arista was also, Jason knew, the public relations director at Doctors Circle. She'd organized a press
conference for him last fall to announce his appointment
to this position.

Sitting across the desk from her, he recommended in
vitro fertilization, which she hadn't yet tried. "It's a lot
simpler than it used to be," Jason said. "We no longer
have to perform surgery. Both the egg retrieval and the
implantation are out-patient procedures."

"That's good." Loretta hugged herself defensively.
She had short, dark hair with a vivid white streak in the
front.

"It's basically a three-week procedure." Jason pro-
duced a brochure to illustrate his words. "For two
weeks, you'll be intensively prepped with hormones."

When the eggs were ripe, they would be removed with
a needle under local anesthesia and grown in a laboratory for several days. After fertilization with her husband's sperm, they would be implanted in her womb.
The odds of a pregnancy resulting were about one in
four.

"That means a 75 percent chance of failure, doesn't

it?'' Loretta explained that her sister, Rita, was pregnant with triplets, which only made her more eager to have a child herself.

"I understand." Jason was pleased to see from her file that Loretta had been seeing the staff counselor to deal with the emotional fallout of infertility. "Have you and your husband considered adoption?"

"We already went through the home-study process, but I understand it's difficult to find an infant," Loretta said. "Besides, I'm not ready to adopt yet. Can my eggs be ready when the embryologist comes on board in two weeks?"

"The timing looks good. Let's set up our next appointment and we'll get started," Jason said.

"Thanks, Doctor. Is it okay if I put on my public relations hat now?"

"Of course." He grinned at the metaphor.

Loretta visibly relaxed, becoming more animated as she switched gears. "I want to photograph you in the new facility when it's closer to completion. I'll need to interview you and the embryologist for a press kit, too."

"Just let my secretary know what day would be convenient," he said.

After she left, Edith appeared. "Can you help her?"

"I hope so," he said. "Wait, don't say it. I know we have to keep the love flowing around here."

His nurse chuckled. "You got that right."

The rest of the day flew by, with patients lined up for appointments. Many, he concluded after reviewing their charts, were candidates for the latest techniques. Like Loretta, most couldn't wait to start.

After work, Jason stopped by the supermarket. Having transferred his few possessions to his new home yesterday, he'd been too tired to do more than send out for pizza.

On his way to the checkout stand, a bag of puppy food landed in his cart. One minute he was passing a display of chow, and the next minute there it was, nestled among his selections. Jason nearly put it back, until he told himself that he should give it to the little boys. Maybe it would convince their mother to let them keep Frodo.

At the town house, he stowed the puppy food near the washing machine and fixed himself a meal of rotisserie chicken, mashed potatoes and salad. Afterward, silence settled over the town house like a shroud. He hadn't realized how much larger this place was than the bachelor flat he'd leased in Virginia.

Jason threw on a light jacket and went out for a walk. What a peaceful place this was, he reflected as he admired the lavender azaleas and orange-and-purple birds of paradise. As he passed one unit after another, he heard the murmur of voices and the clink of pots and pans.

When he was growing up, his mother had often missed dinner while selling houses and his father, a doctor, had frequently worked late, too. Still, they'd made a point of dining together two or three times a week.

Meals were meant to be sociable. Jason shoved his hands into his pockets and hurried on.

On the far side of the pool and spa enclosure, he heard yipping noises coming from one of the units. Jason didn't even have to think about it. He walked right up and knocked on the door.

It was answered by the older boy he'd met on Sunday. "I don't suppose Frodo's still for sale, is he?" he heard himself ask.

"I thought you weren't allowed to have pets," the boy replied.

Did the kid have to have such a good memory? "I'm not," he said. "I was asking for a friend."

The boy's father came to the door and introduced himself as Gordon Gray. While they were shaking hands, a small black-and-tan whirlwind flung itself at Jason, leaping at him until he couldn't resist picking it up. His reward was to have his chin sandpapered by an eager tongue.

After he explained that he was considering buying the pup but was concerned about leaving it alone all day, the man said, "My wife, Alice, runs a service, taking dogs for walks. That way they don't get so lonely."

"It sounds perfect," Jason said.

The dog was still for sale and the price of Alice's service proved reasonable. Jason tried not to think about the fact that he was breaking his newly signed lease by acquiring a pet. After a lifetime spent living by the rules, he figured he was entitled to a minor infraction.

There was also the issue of whether he'd be able to take a dog with him to wherever he might move in the future. Jason decided to worry about that when the time came.

He tucked Frodo inside his jacket, where the pup settled contentedly, and went outside. Some brave soul had ventured out to soak in the spa, he realized when he heard the rumble of the jets. As long as the pool gates were unlocked, he might as well cut through to get back to his place.

Halfway across, Jason came abreast of the spa. Steam formed a pillar in the chilly air, ghostlike beneath the overhead lights.

He broke stride when he spotted the woman lounging

in the water with her eyes half-closed. There was no mistaking that auburn hair or that familiar face. Although most of Heather's shape disappeared beneath the roiling water, her breasts made an impressive appearance in a skimpy bikini bra that more than matched his fevered imaginings of the previous day.

They strained the fabric almost beyond endurance. Almost beyond his endurance, anyway.

Beneath his jacket, Frodo chose that moment to protest his confinement by squirming. The normal complement of two arms and two hands weren't nearly enough to hold one puppy while maintaining a nonchalant attitude, Jason discovered.

Heather's eyes flew open. "Jason? I thought you weren't going to use the pool!"

"I'm not," he said. "I'm just taking a walk."

"Then what are you doing in here?" She frowned at the way he clutched his chest. "Are you all right?"

"Fine," he said. "I'm in kind of a hurry, actually."

"I don't understand. What..." She stopped as a nose poked out of his jacket and a sharp yip disturbed the evening calm. Heather's expression warmed. "What a cute puppy."

Jason would have loved to explain the situation, if he hadn't caught sight of the complex manager studying him from the far side of the pool fence. "I have to ask a favor. Get out of the pool, grab my arm and walk home with me."

"What?" She wasn't smiling anymore.

"Please."

Heather's eyes narrowed. "Is this some kind of joke?"

The dog wiggled. The manager opened the gate, although she appeared more curious than disapproving.

Perhaps she merely intended to greet them. On the other hand, Jason might be about to get busted before he even carried his new pet home.

"I'm smuggling," Jason said. "You don't want this poor little puppy to end up at the animal shelter, do you?" Okay, so he was exaggerating. Surely it was justified under the circumstances?

After an excruciating pause, Heather climbed out into the chilly air. Shivering, she reached for the towel she'd left on the concrete.

In the moment before she wrapped it around herself, he glimpsed her nipped-in waist and flat stomach with its teasing navel. A tiny butterfly tattoo barely above the panty line sent a memory flashing through Jason's brain. Although brief, it was unmistakable.

He's seen those parts of Heather before. Her naked waist, her navel and a whole lot more.

So nothing had happened, had it? She owed him an explanation, and he couldn't wait to hear it.

Chapter Five

Inside his living room, Jason closed the door against the cool February air. Although he hadn't turned on the heater, it felt warm.

"I'll get you a fresh towel so you don't catch a chill." He awaited her response, half hoping Heather would peel off her old towel in front of him so he could enjoy the sight of her bikini again—and, with luck, summon up even more pleasurable memories.

With her red hair in a tangle and her face scrubbed, she looked barely out of her teens. Now that the sight of her had unlocked whatever door had been holding back the memories, a vivid sensual impression flooded Jason. He remembered holding her small, lush body tightly to his, her nipples against his chest.

An intense longing stirred inside him. He was ready to do it all again. More than ready. Especially since, to his frustration, he still couldn't recall the incredible release of joining with her.

"I'm not staying." Clutching the oversized terry-cloth wrap, Heather glared at him. "Why on earth would a man who can't bear to waste time planting flowers get a dog?"

He lowered the struggling puppy to the carpet. Its tiny

legs were windmilling so fast that, as soon as it touched down, Frodo shot forward and smacked into the sofa.

The puppy whimpered, then picked itself up and began sniffing around. Jason kept a wary eye on its hind legs. "I've wanted a dog since I was a kid."

Frodo set off in the direction of the kitchen. Jason followed, with Heather trailing behind. "Why didn't you have a dog when you were little?"

"My parents didn't like animals. They wanted our house to look like a showplace."

"My brother and I had a dog, three stray cats and uncounted hamsters," Heather said in her soft, musical voice. "I never knew how lucky I was."

"I was an only child and spent a lot of time with nannies." Although he'd wished for a live-in playmate, Jason had accepted loneliness as a normal part of life. "My parents let me have a goldfish but after it died, I decided not to risk getting another one."

In the kitchen, Frodo poked around the table, licking up crumbs that must have spilled at dinner. Jason imagined he could read Heather's mind as she watched the scene. *You moved in yesterday and you've already got food all over the floor?* On the other hand, maybe she looked so severe because she was cold.

"I'll fix hot chocolate." Without waiting for a reply, he grabbed a box of mix from a grocery sack, which he hadn't emptied after his shopping expedition, and found two mugs in the cabinet.

"I guess I'm not familiar with the nesting habits of the American bachelor," Heather said. "Is it customary to leave your purchases in the bag until you use them?"

"Sure. Not the ice cream, though." He was glad to hear that Heather didn't hang out with a lot of bachelors.

"Aren't you the same Dr. Carmichael who told me

he's a stickler for organization?'' A freckle wrinkled on her nose as she spoke.

"That was different,'' Jason said. "At work, I'm a scientist. At home, I like to take it easy.''

"In *my* town house complex.'' Obviously, she still hadn't gotten over her pique at his decision to rent nearby.

"It's a nice area,'' he said. "The place came furnished, too. And I'll bet the puppy will enjoy my courtyard.''

The puppy. He'd bought a dog to keep in a rental. What on earth was he thinking? Yet already Jason looked forward to Sunday mornings with the two of them relaxing companionably on the couch.

Frodo chose that moment to approach the counter and squat. "Jason!'' Heather cried.

"Get the sliding door!'' He grabbed the puppy, she wrenched open the courtyard door and out went Frodo, barely in time. Had there been a moment's hesitation on either person's part, the result would have been a mess.

Jason chuckled as the dog initiated the ficus tree. "You and I make a great team. We should perform surgery together someday.''

"I'm sure we will, although I hope under more hygienic circumstances.'' Heather gave a disbelieving headshake. "I do want to learn some of the newer surgical techniques from you, although I don't consider today a good test of how well we perform together.'' Once Frodo padded inside, she closed the glass door.

"Of course, this isn't the first time we performed together.'' Summoned by the microwave's bell, Jason removed the two cups of steaming chocolate.

"Excuse me?'' Despite her sternness, Heather had a

cute way of cocking her head as she waited to pounce on his answer.

Jason handed her a mug. Although he suspected it might be risky to run afoul of Heather when she had a hot liquid handy, he couldn't let her stand there freezing to death.

"I have a terrific visual memory," he said.

"I'm sure that comes in handy when you're learning a new procedure." She sipped the cocoa and watched him suspiciously.

"It helps." He leaned against the counter. In the utility bay, Frodo found a T-shirt that had fallen from atop the washing machine and flopped onto it, panting. "Seeing you in your bikini helped me remember what happened in Atlanta."

"I told you, nothing happened."

"Oh, really? Your body says otherwise."

If he'd been worried about Heather catching a chill, his fears vanished as steam all but poured from her ears. Jason could have sworn her towel was starting to glow, too. "My body says nothing! Especially to you!"

"The butterfly," he said.

"What butterfly?"

"The one tattooed right below your navel," he said. "With the wings barely open."

"It symbolizes rebirth. Second chances." Despite Heather's indifferent shrug, her fiery coloring betrayed an agitated state of mind. "So what?"

"I saw it before." Jason made a low, suggestive humming noise. "If I'm not mistaken, I kissed it."

"There's one on my buttocks, too," she snapped. "You can kiss that one if you want."

"No, there isn't." Jason pretended not to notice the

insult. "I'd remember if there were. Now, why don't you come clean about what we did that night?"

A half-dozen expressions from embarrassment to outrage flitted across her face before her mouth twisted in resignation. "All right. It isn't what you think."

"Something tells me we'd better hold the rest of this conversation sitting down." He gestured her into the living room, leaving behind the dozing dog and their empty mugs. After spreading a fresh towel on the couch to soak up the dampness from her swimsuit, he said, "Make yourself comfortable."

"As if I could possibly be comfortable anywhere in your vicinity," Heather muttered.

"I see we're taking the gloves off." Jason took the armchair. "Although, as I recall, you removed a lot more than gloves."

"I'll admit, I didn't tell you the whole story." Heather perched on the sofa with her legs curled beneath her, perhaps because she was so short they barely reached the floor. "I saw no point in going into detail, especially after your unfeeling comment the next morning."

"I apologize for my crankiness," Jason said. "Proceed."

Heather wrapped her arms around herself. Since the towel had slipped, the gesture had the effect of plumping up her already ample breasts. "Which part don't you remember?"

"If I knew that, it would mean I remembered," he pointed out.

"Do you have to be so annoyingly logical?" Her full lips pursed. They ought to be kissed, Jason thought.

"That's what I do best," he said. "Start at the beginning. That way you're less likely to skip anything."

"I'll run through it quickly." As Heather shifted position, a bare leg appeared from beneath the towel. Slim and well-shaped, it had a light sprinkling of freckles that begged to be traced, like a sensuous connect-the-dots puzzle that led all the way up her thighs.

"No hurry." Jason leaned back, arms folded behind his head. He hoped she wouldn't examine his body too closely or she might spot a telltale bulge. On the other hand, if she were interested enough to focus her attention on that part of his anatomy, it might be a promising start.

She believed in second chances, after all. The butterfly testified to it.

"We met at registration in the lobby," Heather said.

"I'm with you so far."

"While we were waiting in line, we talked about one of the seminars we both planned to attend," she said. "The speaker had written an article for the *Medical Journal*. As I recall, we were both skeptical about his methodology."

"A truly romantic topic, one guaranteed to make two hearts beat as one," Jason joked. "No wonder we hit it off."

"I liked your indignation that the man would recommend a surgical procedure that you didn't consider thoroughly tested." She smiled wryly. "You said doctors shouldn't treat women like guinea pigs."

"It's my best pickup line."

"I'll bet you try it on all the girls," she shot back.

"I'm not kidding. It really is my best pickup line," Jason said. "As it happens, though, you're the only woman I've ever tried it on."

"I'm honored." Heather brushed a speck of lint off her arm. The movement loosened her towel enough to reveal a wink from her navel.

Jason's body revved again. He stretched his legs in

Heather's direction. If she uncoiled, he could make contact with her ankles.

She closed the towel and drew herself up more tightly than ever. "We continued our discussion during the welcome reception."

"Where I had a couple of drinks," Jason filled in.

"At the time, they didn't affect you, or so it appeared," Heather said. "Since I'd never met you before, I didn't realize your affable manner indicated you verged on becoming comatose."

"I'm affable now," he pointed out.

She looked away as if searching for a sharp answer. When none came, she continued, "We decided to order a late dinner from room service."

"Steak and eggs." Jason could still taste it. "You had salad and half my slice of chocolate cake."

"I'll bet that's the only time in your life you ever shared your dessert," Heather said.

She was right. "Score one for your side."

"Am I ahead?"

"We're tied."

She didn't argue. "The next thing I knew, our clothes were on the floor and we were on the bed."

"All of our clothes?" Abandoning his casual pose, Jason leaned forward eagerly.

"Almost all."

"Which ones weren't?"

"Could we just get on with the story, please?" Heather asked.

He decided not to press the issue. "If you insist."

"We reached a point at which we mutually decided that I should retrieve some birth control from my purse," Heather said.

Although he knew he shouldn't interrupt the flow of

narrative, this statement raised several obvious questions. "You carry it around with you? So I wasn't your first case of, er, spontaneous clothes-shedding?"

"I'm leaving." Heather unfolded her legs. The exquisite view wasn't enough to distract Jason from the realization that he'd offended her.

"I'm sorry. I didn't mean it the way it came out," he said. "After your comment about not having much experience in bachelors' kitchens, it surprises me that you carry birth control in your purse. That's all."

To his relief, Heather settled back against the cushions. "I believe in taking precautions. I should think you'd approve, after that comment you made about my nurse."

"I do approve." He deserved the rebuke, Jason acknowledged.

Heather appeared mollified. "Don't forget that I work with teen mothers in the Moms in Training Program. I have to set a good example for them by being prepared, whether I expect to need it or not. Now, do you want to hear the rest of the story?"

"Avidly," Jason said.

"It took me a minute to dig through my purse," Heather went on. "When I travel, I carry a lot."

"No surprise there."

"By the time I got back, you were asleep." Her eyebrows flicked upward in an end-of-story expression.

"That's it?" He couldn't believe he'd been such an oaf.

"More or less."

"What's the 'more' part?"

"The next morning," she said.

"You're referring to my rude comment about hoping I wouldn't hear any more about it?" Jason said. "I apologize. My head was pounding, but that's no excuse. I really am sorry."

"You should be."

He did his best to look ashamed, and succeeded for about five seconds. "Any chance of our picking up where we left off?"

"Jason!"

"I didn't mean that. Well, yes, I did." Deep inside, a voice warned that the last thing he needed was to get involved with a colleague. Especially one who wanted a yard filled with roses. Being a man, however, meant that certain parts of Jason's brain were subject to whiteout on occasion.

"There's only one thing I want from you," Heather said.

He had a feeling it wasn't mind-altering, bedroom-demolishing sex. "What's that?"

"Closure." Her fingers tapped impatiently on what appeared to be her knees, although he couldn't be sure because they were hidden by the towel. "An acknowledgement that nothing ultimately happened, and an end to your questions."

"Done." In the absence of any evidence to the contrary, he saw no reason to doubt her word.

A tap on the door made them both start. In case it was the manager, Jason cast a quick glance toward the kitchen. No sign of Frodo, who was probably fast asleep.

"Do you want me to wait in the other room?" Heather asked in a low voice. "It could be embarrassing if someone saw me like this."

"Or it could do wonders for my reputation," he teased. "Don't worry about it."

As he opened the door, a young, dark-haired woman

raised her fist to knock again. She nearly rapped on his chest. "Oops."

"No harm done." She must be one of his neighbors, Jason figured, spotting a baby stroller behind her. "What can I do for you?"

"I'm looking for…"

"Olive!" Heather hurried to the door. "Jason, this is my niece that I mentioned, the one who's staying with me."

"Hi, niece." The two certainly had dissimilar coloring, he mused. If he hadn't known she and Heather were related, he'd never have guessed.

"Jason?" The young woman examined him with interest. "Jason Carmichael?"

"That would be me," he said.

"I mentioned you to her," Heather explained. To Olive, she said, "I ran into him at the spa."

The young woman held out a cell phone. "You left this at the house. I know you always carry it with you, so I took it to the pool. When I saw you weren't there, I followed the trail."

"Trail?" Heather said.

"You dripped all over the place." Her niece shrugged. "Sorry I interrupted you."

"I was just leaving."

"Don't hurry on my account," Olive said.

"That's all right." Heather edged past Jason toward the door.

"At least let me provide a dry towel. I'll be happy to launder that one for you and bring it over later." He didn't really expect her to accept his offer, but he'd love an excuse to drop by.

"You didn't tell me he was such a gentleman, um,

Aunt Heather,'' said the young woman. Jason wondered why she stumbled over the word *aunt*.

"He isn't a gentleman. However, we do have to work together," Heather announced. "I'm afraid he and I may have gotten off on the wrong foot."

If we'd stayed on our feet, there'd be nothing to argue about. Although Jason abstained from blurting out the tactless remark, he suspected from Heather's quelling look that she had a good idea of what he was thinking. "Since I gather your aunt isn't accepting my offer, I'll just say that it was nice to meet you, Olive, and wish you both a pleasant walk home."

From the stroller came a fussing noise. Heather hurried past the young woman and scooped up a baby warmly dressed in a blanket sleeper.

The infant, about five or six months old, peeked sleepily at Jason. She had a Little Orphan Annie tangle of curls the same shade as Heather's.

The infant resembled her great-aunt more than her own mother. Heredity could certainly be unpredictable.

"Cute kid," he said.

"Her name's Ginger." Olive smiled.

"It suits her." It seemed to Jason that Ginger studied him at unusual length for so young a child. "She's very bright."

"Brilliant!" Heather said.

"Yes, well, gr…great-aunts tend to be partial," Olive said. "It's true, though."

"Don't keep her out in the cold. I mean your aunt." Heather was shivering, Jason noticed. "She could catch a chill."

"See you in the morning." With that, his colleague turned and, still holding Ginger, left her niece to push the empty stroller behind her down the walkway.

Something didn't ring right about that scenario, Jason reflected as he closed the door. Unable to put his finger on exactly what he suspected, however, he gave up and went to set out food and water for Frodo.

"YOUR NIECE?" Olive demanded as Heather hurried into the warmth of the town house. "I understand that you don't want people gossiping at work, but this pretense will be hard to maintain. The guy's going to be our neighbor."

"I didn't know that when I lied to him." Her arms bumpy from the cold, Heather climbed the stairs with Ginger in her arms. "Besides, you'll only be here for another three weeks."

"That's true." Her daughter followed. "You know something? I don't know how you can deny that he likes you."

"He likes to tease me," Heather said. "I don't understand why. At work, he's got a reputation as a tyrant." Going into the guest bedroom, she laid the baby in her portable crib. "I hope I didn't get her damp. She looked so adorable, I couldn't resist holding her."

Olive ran her hands over the sleeper to check. "She's fine. And it's okay, Mom. I know you're going through separation anxiety because we're moving out."

"Separation anxiety?" Heather hadn't expected to hear such a technical term from her daughter. It was hard to remember that Olive had earned a degree in psychology. "I suppose so."

From her bedroom, Heather fetched her robe and went into the bathroom to change. Olive waited outside, clearly not finished discussing Jason Carmichael. "I think a romance is what you need," she called through the door. "It'll help you forget that I'm leaving."

"A romance?" Uh-oh. "Don't get ideas. Jason is not husband material."

"How do you know?"

"I've heard rumors." Female physicians shared war stories at conventions, particularly when it came to a good-looking bachelor like Dr. Carmichael.

"What kind of rumors?" demanded Olive.

"He was engaged to a woman in Boston. A former colleague of his said he dumped the woman without warning." Heather hadn't found out about this until several months after her own encounter with the man. "He abruptly took another post and moved to England."

Hearing how he'd abandoned his fiancée had made Heather so angry she'd wondered if she could ever speak to Jason again, even on business. She'd had to remind herself that he wasn't Ned and that the woman, as far as she knew, hadn't been pregnant.

Stripped of her wet clothes and warmly wrapped at last, she tried to restore some semblance of order to her hair. It sprang up defiantly. She hated to think what a witch she'd looked like in front of Jason, not that she cared what he thought of her.

"Maybe he had his reasons." Although Olive sounded dubious, she clearly hated to give up on such an intriguing possibility as a match for Heather. "He's awfully cute."

"I doubt his secretary thinks so. He's always chewing her out." He'd only scolded Coral once, as far as Heather knew, but she wanted to rid her daughter of this crazy notion about a romance.

"Maybe she needs to shape up."

"Olive!"

"Okay, okay. I'm sure he's a mean old ogre and his secretary is the sweetest thing since pecan pie." When

Heather emerged from the bathroom, Olive greeted her with a hug. "I suppose I'm worried about you, now that I'm leaving."

Heather hugged her in return, relishing their closeness. "Why on earth?"

"Because I'll have John and Ginger, while you'll be alone," her daughter said.

"I've handled it fine all these years. Besides, I hope you'll settle nearby." From her daughter's hesitation, Heather gathered there was something she hadn't been told. "What?"

"John wants to join his father's insurance business in Texas," Olive said. "I was waiting for the right time to tell you."

"There is no right time." Heather struggled to hide her disappointment. She hadn't even been aware, herself, of how much she'd been counting on watching her granddaughter grow up day by day. "Don't worry about me. You two have to make your own plans, and this sounds like a good one."

"We'd love to have you visit as often as you can," Olive said. "Oh, and Mom?"

"Yes?" Heather hoped she wasn't going to be treated to any more painful revelations.

"I want to invite my grandfather to the wedding, too." She was referring to her grandfather by adoption, Heather gathered. "I'm sure he'd love to be there. I wasn't thinking straight after John called or I'd have included him in the first place."

Heather was ashamed to realize she'd been feeling sorry for herself when there were so many other people who loved Olive and were going to miss her, too. "That's a great idea. And you know what? I'm just grateful I've had this time with you and Ginger. It's been special.''

"I'm grateful, too,'' said her daughter, and hugged her again.

Chapter Six

During the next two weeks, Olive's guest list grew by leaps and bounds. First an aunt and uncle also needed to be included, then John's grandparents and brothers. Olive decided to add her best friend Julia as maid of honor, as well.

The town house became a jumble of catalogs and wedding gifts. Heather was so busy she didn't have time to soak in the spa and, mercifully, Jason didn't invite himself over.

She knew he was putting in long hours at work, handling administrative details and hiring staff as well as seeing patients. The opening of the Infertility Center was now less than a month away, although the official hoopla would wait until May to coincide with the conclusion of the Endowment Fund Drive.

"I'm relieved that there hasn't been any blood on the walls," Natalie Barr said one Monday as she and Heather ate lunch with Amy at the remodeled cafeteria in the Birthing Center. The once-drab walls had been repainted mint green and the long tables replaced by more intimate settings. "From you and Jason fighting, I mean."

"Why should there be?" Although Heather had told

her friends about Olive and Ginger, she hadn't confided anything about Atlanta.

"You know how the stories went around after he was named director instead of you." After tucking an errant strand of black hair into her French braid, Amy dug her fork into her pasta primavera.

"I knew you didn't resent his appointment," Natalie said. "But you're both so hard-nosed, I figured you'd clash over everything."

"He's been busy. We haven't had time to talk much these past few weeks." The lack of interaction with Jason had left Heather unsettled. She found herself watching for him at the town house and glancing up whenever someone walked by her office. "I'm sure we'll have our disagreements from time to time, but we're both professionals. We'll work things out."

"With daggers?" Natalie asked.

"Flaming e-mails?" Amy suggested.

"Nothing of the kind." Heather finished another bite of spinach salad before adding, "We're both reasonable people."

Natalie hooted. "We know how mild-mannered you are when you're aroused, Heather! Jason, too."

"I've been known to speak my mind," she conceded. "As for him, it's time he learned to control his temper."

"Speaking up is healthier than letting your resentments simmer," Amy said. "Although of course people need to be considerate."

"Oh!" With a clink, Natalie dropped her fork.

"What's wrong?" Concern wiped away all other thoughts for Heather. Natalie's baby wasn't due for another two months. If she'd begun labor this early, she needed treatment immediately.

The mother-to-be rubbed her side. "Bun kicked me in the ribs."

"Bun?" Heather repeated.

"You're not going to name the poor kid Bunny, are you?" Amy asked. They both knew Natalie collected rabbit memorabilia.

Nat kept one hand on her abdomen for a moment before lifting it away. Apparently the movements had subsided. "No. We're considering Melissa if it's a girl and Joseph if it's a boy."

"That's so sweet!" Heather said.

Joseph Barr, Natalie's husband's late father, had founded Doctors Circle in memory of his first child, a daughter named Melissa who'd been stillborn. Joe had been convinced that, with better medical care, the baby might have survived. His hard work and dedication had ensured that the women of Serene Beach would never go without proper prenatal care again.

"The names were no problem." Natalie's expression sobered. "I just wish I could say the same for…" She broke off as a couple of young women walked by. Heather recognized one as a receptionist who was a notorious gossip.

After the pair set down their trays at a table across the room, Amy said, "What's going on?"

"Nothing." Realizing her friends weren't buying it, Natalie said, "Well, okay, I'm a little worried about the Endowment Fund and I prefer not to have the entire staff know it."

After Joe Barr's death, the hospital's administrator had made a mess of the finances. Joe's son Patrick, a pediatrician, had left his practice to take over and had soon returned the medical center to financial stability.

However, to ensure the center's financial future and

protect his father's dream, he'd launched a thirty-million-dollar fund drive last fall in a symbolic nine-month campaign. Of the goal, ten million dollars had been raised quickly and another ten million in matching funds had been promised in December.

"How short are we?" Heather asked.

"About eight million," Natalie said.

"There's two months to go," Amy pointed out. "Loretta mentioned a fund-raising ball next month. That ought to help."

"Eight million dollars sounds like such an incredible amount of money." Natalie had grown up on the poor side of town, one of five children. "I still feel weird spending more than a hundred dollars for a dress, but how else am I going to attend society events with Patrick?"

"I'll bet you're the most beautiful woman there," Amy said loyally.

"And the most fun to be around," Heather added.

Natalie, who never stayed downhearted for long, grinned at her friends. "You guys are great for my ego."

A soft throat-clearing made them all look up. Coral Liu gave an apologetic smile. "I'm sorry to interrupt. Dr. Carmichael asked me to tell Dr. Rourke he'd like to speak with her."

Didn't the man know she was eating lunch? Heather wondered grumpily. Perhaps not, in all fairness. George Farajian of the Ob/Gyn Department was still making out her schedule as well as arranging her weekends and evenings on call.

"Can't it wait?" Natalie asked.

"It's okay. I need to diet, anyway." The last thing Heather wanted was to put Coral in a bad light with her boss.

After bidding her friends good-bye, Heather was heading to the West Wing when Coral shook her head. "He's in his new office," the secretary said.

No wonder Jason had been virtually invisible recently, Heather mused. "I didn't realize it was ready."

"The rest of the clinic isn't, but he wanted to settle in as quickly as possible," Coral explained.

"The king's in a hurry to stake out his kingdom," Heather murmured.

"Excuse me?"

"Nothing," she said. "You don't have to escort me, Coral. It's probably your lunch hour, too."

"It's better if I come along," the young woman said. "In case there's anything else he needs."

They hurried across the courtyard, past staff members eating at the round tables near the fountain. "You must have a lot of patience to put up with him the way you do."

"I'm as much a perfectionist as he is," Coral said.

"Have you always worked for doctors?"

"Oh, no." Despite her slim build, the young woman walked with a quick step. "I used to assist the vice-president of a company that makes replacement parts for oil wells. I decided I'd be happier working somewhere that I cared about the product."

"And in this case, the product is babies," Heather observed.

Coral nodded. "I don't have any children myself. I'm not sure whether I want them. Still, they make other women very happy. I suppose oil wells make people happy, too, but it isn't the same."

"You can't hug a gusher or sing it a lullaby," Heather said. "On the other hand, you don't have to change its diaper in the middle of the night, either."

The secretary giggled. "You have a funny sense of humor."

"So does Dr. Carmichael," Heather said, "although I don't suppose you see that side of him."

Amazement made Coral miss her stride. "Dr. Carmichael? He seems very serious."

Heather decided not to describe how ridiculous he'd looked smuggling a puppy inside his jacket. "Once in a while he breaks down and does a fair imitation of a human."

Coral started to smile, then brought her features under control. Heather had to admire her sense of loyalty, or perhaps it was abject fear.

Inside the clinic, the flooring felt springy underfoot and the walls reeked of fresh paint. She heard voices in the lab, probably workmen installing equipment under the watchful eye of the new embryologist, Eric Wong, Ph.D.

Coral spared a wistful glance in that direction. Heather wondered if there was more than one kind of chemistry going on in that laboratory, and decided it was none of her business.

Having entered through the main atrium, they passed unfurnished examining rooms en route to the offices in the back. "I would have brought you through the side door but it was just painted this morning," Coral said.

"That's okay. I like to see how the place is coming along." She hadn't yet selected an office, Heather recalled with a guilty twinge.

In an anteroom, a desk and file drawers testified to the fact that Coral was already working here. She tapped at the inner door. "Dr. Carmichael? I've brought Dr. Rourke."

"Send her in." Jason sounded distracted and gruff.

Heather could understand how he might be intimidating, at least to a woman who hadn't seen him nearly naked. Come to think of it, he'd been impressive in that state, too.

She entered. "What can I do for you?"

There was no sign of the puppy-smuggling rascal in the man who glanced at her from behind his desk. He was standing, as if too impatient to sit, with a couple of open files spread in front of him.

Legs apart and muscular arms braced on his desk, he might have been a general planning a dangerous campaign. Taped to the walls, flow charts and schedules gave the office the appearance of a war room.

"Hang on a minute." Jason made a note on a sheet of paper. Heather registered the newly laid carpet, the large desk with a computer blinking on its return arm, and the neatly arranged shelves. It was quite well-organized for a man who didn't bother to unbag his groceries, but then, he didn't have his secretary to help at home.

"Will there be anything else, Dr. Carmichael?" Coral asked.

"I said, hang on!" The edge to his tone made his secretary flinch.

"I could have finished my lunch if I'd known you weren't ready to talk to me," Heather said.

He looked up. A couple of blinks later, her point sank in. "You were at lunch?"

Coral tensed as if she feared another rebuke simply for following his orders. "I don't mind," Heather said. "I knew you might not be aware of my schedule." *And if you bark at your secretary on my account, I'll throw something at you.*

Her silent threat must have communicated itself to

Jason or perhaps he remembered his manners. All he said was, "I apologize, Doctor. Thanks, Coral, I don't need anything else."

The secretary left. Heather could almost hear her sigh of relief.

"What's going on?" she said.

"First, I wanted to let you know about the two new specialists who'll be joining us." He handed over two résumés. "You can read those at your leisure. Also, unless you have any objections, I'm assigning you the other corner office. It's the next biggest one after mine and it meets your specifications."

"My specifications?" Oh, yes. "It's on the far end of the corridor."

He almost smiled. In Jason's present state of mind, she suspected his face might crack if his mouth stretched any further. "You can start moving in on Friday, if you like."

"I'll be out of town on Friday." It was, amazingly, time for Olive's wedding.

His brow furrowed. "No one informed me."

"I didn't think of it," Heather admitted. "George made out my schedule and arranged for someone to cover when I'm away."

Jason indicated one of the wall charts. "Our schedule won't start until next month, but in future please consult with me before taking time off."

"Yes, sir." She stifled the impulse to salute.

"Anything interesting?" he asked.

"I'm sorry?"

"Where you're going," Jason said. "For your long weekend. Not that I'm being nosy. I just wondered where people go for vacations around here."

"Las Vegas." Not wanting him to suspect her of a

gambling problem, Heather added, "I'm attending a wedding."

"I see." He lost interest immediately, she could tell from his expression. "Oh, one more thing."

"Yes?"

"From now on, our focus will be strictly on our infertility patients. I realize you're seeing some general patients, and I want you to start transferring them to other doctors." Jason's brisk tone implied that of course she would comply.

Heather nearly dropped the two resumés. "Some women get very upset at having to change doctors."

"You've only been at Doctors Circle for three years." Obviously, he'd looked up her background. "It's not as if you have elderly patients who've been with you all their lives."

"That's true, but some of them were distressed when their last doctor left," Heather pointed out. "They're finally starting to feel comfortable again."

"I don't want your loyalties divided between the needs of the Infertility Clinic and the demands of your old practice," Jason said.

Heather fought down her instinct to defy him. Although his high-handedness irked her, she needed to weigh his position. Perhaps he had a point, although right now she had a hard time accepting it.

"I'm scheduled to deliver Natalie Barr's baby. She's due in May," she said. "I hope you're not going to insist that I hand her over to someone else." Surely even Jason Carmichael wouldn't force her to abandon the administrator's wife.

"Fine. I'll make an exception for Mrs. Barr." Jason snapped a file shut. "As I mentioned, we've got two additional physicians joining us next month. The same rules have to apply to everyone. We can see our infertility patients through to delivery, but we refer routine exams and non-infertility problems to Ob/Gyn.''

"I see." How could a man be so quick to bend the rules when it came to his lease and so rigid about his department? Perhaps that wasn't a fair question, Heather knew, but she was in no mood to cut Jason any slack. "If there's nothing else, I'll be going."

"Thanks for stopping in." His cell phone rang, and as she let herself out of the office, Jason was already absorbed in his conversation.

"Did it go all right?" Coral asked in a low voice.

Heather closed the door behind her. "Next time, I'll wear body armor. I hope this job is worth what they're paying you."

"It is," Coral said. "I just hope I make it through probation."

"You're on probation?" That possibility hadn't occurred to Heather.

"For three months," the secretary said.

"Who decides whether you pass?" Heather hoped it was Dr. Barr.

"Dr. Carmichael." Coral tapped her fingers nervously on her desk. "I'm doing everything I can to please him."

"Let's hope he appreciates it."

Heather was still simmering when she reached the Ob/Gyn Department. George Farajian caught sight of her from where he stood by the nurses' station. "Problems?" he asked.

"Grrr," Heather said.

The department head steered Heather into his comfortable office. "If it's about Dr. Carmichael's request that you divest yourself of non-infertility patients, he already told me about it.''

"I feel as though I'm abandoning them," she said.

"The women will be disappointed, but surely they can sympathize with those who are desperate to have babies," he said.

"You mean I should make them feel guilty because they don't want to give up their doctor?" Heather asked.

George chuckled sympathetically. "I didn't look at it that way. But it seems a waste to have you giving women their annual checkups when infertility patients need your attention.''

"I suppose so." Heather enjoyed all the aspects of her work, though. "I find it reassuring to treat some women who aren't having problems, because I'm a woman, too. It reminds me that most of the time nature functions the way it's supposed to.''

"I hope you won't find working at the new clinic unduly stressful," the department head said. "However, on the positive side, Jason has assured me that his obstetricians will back us up in a pinch. You know how busy it can get around here.''

"Babies all want to be born at once." Heather had sometimes wondered if there weren't such a thing as a prenatal conspiracy, especially on holidays, weekends and evenings.

"There are bound to be some rough patches as the new clinic gets established," George said. "Although you're more affected than most of us, I'm sure you'll adjust.''

Heather was glad she hadn't blown up at Jason, since her old boss shared his point of view. "Thanks," she said. "I appreciate your positive attitude.''

"How could I be anything but positive when I get to see miracles every day?" said the obstetrician.

Heather felt better. "Sometimes I forget how wonderful this job is."

In her office, she read about the two new doctors who would be arriving. Dr. Alexei Davidoff was a Russian-born reproductive endocrinologist. Gruff but brilliant was the impression Heather had formed on hearing him speak once at a seminar.

She'd never met the second new staff member, Dr. Lisa Arcadian. The woman had trained in England at the same institute where Jason had worked. He'd left his fiancée to go there, Heather recalled.

In her photograph, the young woman had a sparkling smile and thick, dark-blond hair. Heather nearly choked as it struck her that there might be more between Jason and Lisa Arcadian than mere professional respect.

She was absurdly pleased to note at the bottom of the sheet that Lisa was married to a Dr. Henry Arcadian. Heather's stomach untwisted.

What was wrong with her? she wondered. She didn't want to be jealous of Jason. Yet he kept sneaking into her thoughts when she least expected it. He'd been so warm and cuddly at his town house that he'd reminded her of why she'd nearly gone to bed with him in the first place. Well, if anyone ought to know how charming a man could be one minute and how rejecting the next, it was Heather.

The phone rang. It was the charge nurse at Labor and Delivery to tell her one of her patients had just been admitted.

Heather sprang to her feet, fired with energy. Another miracle was on its way.

THE MEETING with Heather had gone well, Jason thought. He'd expected her to put up more of a fight about relinquishing her non-infertility patients.

He couldn't understand why anyone would want to hang on to routine appointments with such an exciting clinic on the verge of opening. Simply walking through the unfinished premises set his mind whirring with plans and possibilities.

The excellence of his new staff members meant a further boost to the clinic's public image. Patrick Barr had told Jason that their reputations, combined with his, were definitely a help with the fund-raising.

But medicine was as much an art as a science. Heather's clinical experience and rapport with clients should prove as important to the clinic's success as Lisa and Alexei's lists of credentials.

Jason had missed her these past few weeks, from the liveliness of her bright face to her spicy fragrance with its hint of baby powder. Several times, he'd dropped by the whirlpool bath in the evenings, but he'd seen no sign of her.

Last weekend, he'd even gone to her town house, seeking advice on how to keep Frodo from chewing on his socks. When he'd reached it, however, the front door had stood open and, from inside, he'd heard several women discussing a wedding dinner. Not wanting to interrupt when Heather had company, he'd withdrawn before anyone spotted him.

He knew it was best to stay out of her life. Why, then, did he keep dreaming of a butterfly waiting for his touch?

Jason's stride carried him through the March sunshine and across to the West Wing, where he was continuing to see his patients until the new examining rooms were completed. On the second floor, his nurse tapped her foot as she waited for him.

"Am I late?" He checked the wall clock and answered his own question. "Only by five minutes."

"Mrs. LoBianco is an important patient," Edith informed him. "Her husband made a $5-million donation to the Endowment Fund."

"All my patients are important." Mrs. LoBianco, he'd noted when he reviewed her chart earlier, was thirty-eight. Although she and her husband, computer-gaming magnate Alfred LoBianco, had an eight-year-old daughter, she hadn't been able to get pregnant again.

According to their previous doctor's report, the problem lay not with her but with her husband. Since they had rejected the idea of using a donor, it appeared the couple might benefit from ICSI, or intracytoplasmic sperm injection, in which a single sperm could be injected directly into the egg. It allowed fertilization if the husband had even a few healthy sperm.

"I can tell that woman's nervous about this consultation." Edith fixed him with her dark, knowing eyes. "Don't you go scaring her any more than she already is."

"Me?" Jason took the chart, which she'd been clutching as if undecided whether to let him have it. "I couldn't scare a stray puppy."

"You've got Coral Liu in a state of terror and Heather Rourke ready to pull out that pretty red hair of hers by the roots," his nurse countered.

Heather hadn't been in a particularly bad mood as far as he could tell. "She must have been annoyed that I interrupted her lunch," he said.

"That's not it," Edith assured him. "She growled."

"She did what?"

The nurse made a low snarling noise. "At Dr. Farajian."

"Did she bite him, too?" Jason asked.

"I don't know. She went into his office and that's the last I heard," Edith said. "But if she doesn't calm down, she might need another leave of absence."

"Did you say 'another'?" He hadn't heard anything about Heather going on leave. "When was that?"

"October and November," Edith said promptly.

When Jason had run into Heather last September while visiting Doctors Circle, there'd been no mention of her going on leave. "Why?" he said.

"Nobody knows." Edith shrugged. "Some people thought she was mad because you got the director's job instead of her, but I don't believe it. If you want the truth, you could ask Mrs. Barr or Mrs. Ladd. They're her best friends."

"Thanks." Jason had no intention of prying into Heather's personal business.

Nevertheless, he felt as if there were a puzzle he needed to assemble. The pieces included a cute baby who looked like Heather, a niece who didn't resemble her at all and an unexplained leave of absence right around the time the baby was born.

Puzzling. Of course, he might be making much ado about nothing.

Or maybe not.

Chapter Seven

On Tuesday, after hours, Heather decided to visit a new women's boutique on Bordeaux Way, near Doctors Circle. Several women at work had recommended it.

Although she'd planned to wear a dove-gray suit to Olive's wedding, she impulsively pulled into the parking lot and went inside. She wanted to look her best in the wedding photos that her daughter would keep for the rest of her life.

"Do you carry petites?" she asked the middle-aged saleslady.

"Certainly." The woman sized her up at a glance. "We have several designs I think will be perfect for you." She led the way to a rack at one side.

Flipping through the selections, Heather sighed with approval. The first dress she chose was a vivid wine color edged in black, the second a dramatic midnight blue, the third golden brown. All were designed to flatter figures that were short with a large bust.

In a changing room, Heather tried on the wine-and-black dress first. Although it was hard to tell in the subdued light, she concluded that the hues didn't flatter her delicate skin. Neither did the midnight blue, which was not only the wrong color but also too tight.

"How are you doing?" called the saleslady.

"I'm afraid these are rejects." Heather handed the garments over the dressing-room door. "Two down, one to go."

"Let me see if there's anything in the back room," the woman said. "We get new shipments all the time and they haven't all been put on the racks."

The russet gown slipped smoothly into place. The color was perfect, but the neckline dipped a bit low for Heather's taste and a slit up the side revealed a lot of leg. The effect was sexy and daring—and a little alarming.

Since high school, when the pregnancy had given her a reputation of being easy, Heather had preferred to cover up. Regarding herself in this gown, however, brought a surge of rebelliousness. Did she have to keep redeeming herself forever?

Trying to make up her mind, Heather stepped out of the dressing room to examine herself in a full-length mirror she'd seen in the shop. As she was adjusting the top, the front door opened and Jason walked in.

He halted, his gaze raking her with no pretense of subtlety. Surrounded by ladies' finery and frills, his tall form looked more masculine than ever, and his confident stance exuded pure male desire. "Now that's what I call a dress."

Heather became intensely aware of the caress of the fabric against her skin. Her bare leg and low cleavage made her feel both exposed and a little excited.

"I'd hardly expect you to call it anything else," she said tartly. "What brings you to a ladies' dress shop?"

"My mother's birthday is next week. She loves scarves and I heard they carry beautiful ones here." Despite his words, he made no move toward a rack floating with gossamer wisps of silk.

"I'm sure your mother will appreciate it."

Jason cut straight through her attempt at small talk. "You look stunning," he said. "If you wear that to the wedding in Las Vegas, you'll steal the bride's thunder."

Heather had to laugh. "It's not very appropriate for…" She caught herself on the cusp of saying "the mother of the bride." "…a guest, is it?"

"Not unless you want the groom to race from the altar and whisk you to his suite." He delivered this outrageous remark as if it were self-evident. "You know what that dress lacks?"

"Enough yardage?" The more she studied her reflection, the more Heather convinced herself the outfit was too sexy for her taste. Yet it made her feel like a movie star.

"This." From the rack, Jason lifted a diaphanous scarf hand-painted with silver and bronze leaves.

Before Heather could grasp his intent, he strolled to her and draped the fabric around her shoulders. As his fingers brushed her collarbone, sparks arced through her bloodstream.

"I've never been the scarf type," she said.

"It might look better this way." He adjusted the drape at his leisure, seeming to enjoy shifting it as if unaware that each contact with his hands sent sensations flowing all the way to her knees.

Heather knew she ought to protest and snatch the scarf away from him. Instead, she stood transfixed.

The saleswoman returned amid the rustle of fabric. Seeing Jason, she said, "Oh, good, you brought your husband."

The two of them practically leaped apart. "He's not my husband," Heather said. "We work together."

"Dr. Rourke was kind enough to model this scarf. I think my mother would prefer a darker color, though." As Jason turned his attention to the display, Heather noticed that he was breathing hard.

What had come over her? She didn't want Jason handling her! Annoyed at herself, she took the saleslady's find, a lavender cocktail dress with a matching jacket, and returned to the dressing room.

Only when she started to take off the russet gown did Heather realize she still wore the scarf. As she removed it, a whiff of Jason's scent made her quiver all over again.

The dress *was* beautiful. With the scarf, it cast an air of mystery and seduction.

Heather lifted the price tag and winced. Reluctantly setting it aside, she tried on the new arrival.

Where the russet gown might lure a man into bed, the lavender dress was far more suitable to wear to a wedding. The subtle color and the jacket also made the ensemble perfect for those opening-night parties at conventions where suits looked too stiff and everything else too fancy.

She would get lots of use out of it. It would never thrill her the way the russet dress did, though. And there was no scarf to remind her of Jason's touch.

Heather could almost hear her daughter's voice saying, "Buy them both, Mom. You know you can use them."

Her natural thriftiness, reinforced by years of scrimping to pay for medical school, warred with her feminine instincts. Heather resolved the dilemma by reminding herself that, once purchased, the dresses would augment her understocked closet for years.

Besides, she would need more than one gown for the festivities in Las Vegas. Olive and John had arranged for a day of sightseeing and taking in a performance by Cirque de Soleil before the big event so their friends and relatives—the guests now numbered about thirty—could get acquainted.

"I'll take them," she told the woman, and reminded herself again that this was an investment.

When she came out, she found Jason waiting at the counter with a rainbow assortment of scarves. "I couldn't pick just one so I decided to indulge her fantasies," he said, eyeing Heather appreciatively.

The saleslady gave a discreet cough.

"I was referring to my mother," he said calmly.

"Oh, it's a gift? I'll wrap them for you." To Heather, the woman said, "Are you in a hurry?"

"I can wait," she said.

When the clerk disappeared into the back, Jason said, "I'm glad to see you're buying the dress."

"Two of them," she pointed out. "I'm indulging my own fantasies."

"At a wedding?" he asked.

"It's a two-day event," she explained. "We'll be celebrating all over Las Vegas."

He absorbed this information thoughtfully. "So who's going to be there?"

"The bride and groom," she said.

"Who else?"

"No one in particular." She gave the words a lilt, as if to imply that she had an admirer, or several, waiting in the wings.

"Anyone I know?" Before she could answer, the

saleslady returned with a gift-wrapped package. Seeing no chance to buttonhole Heather, he paid, bade them both farewell and departed.

"What a handsome man!" the clerk said.

"And good to his mother." Heather smiled demurely as she signed her credit-card receipt.

It tickled her that Jason had wondered who was going to see her in the russet dress. She couldn't help wondering if she would ever have a chance to wear it for him again. Just to remind him of what he was missing, of course.

ON WEDNESDAY NIGHT, some of Olive's college friends were taking her out for a bachelorette dinner. Heather, who had volunteered to babysit, fixed herself a frozen dinner for the first time in several months.

"Don't tell me that's what you're going to be eating after I move out!" her daughter said as she came downstairs in slacks and a blouse. She looked fresh and glowing, the picture of a happy bride-to-be.

"I don't always have time to cook, and there's not much point when I'm alone." Quickly, Heather added, "Don't you dare read anything into that!"

"You should join some clubs. Go out and meet people," Olive said. "Invite that nice Dr. Carmichael over for dinner."

"I'd rather starve."

Her daughter heaved an exaggerated sigh. "You're telling me it's a coincidence that he moved in nearby and you finally went out and bought yourself some decent clothes?"

Last night, she'd insisted that Heather model the new dresses, which she'd applauded. The two of them were more like sisters than mother and daughter, Heather thought. Who could have guessed that the baby she had relinquished with a heavy heart would someday become her close friend?

"I've got to go," Olive said. "Ginger took a late nap. I doubt she'll be ready for bed until later," she called.

"If it's all right with you, I'll take her to the health club." The facility, located a few blocks away, provided child care until 9:00 p.m. "I'm behind on my work-outs."

"Good idea. A change of scenery ought to help wear her out." Olive stifled a yawn. "I want to get as much sleep as I can tonight and tomorrow. Wouldn't it be awful if John saw me for the first time in months and I had bags under my eyes?"

"Twenty-one-year-olds don't get bags under their eyes," Heather said.

"That's what you think! Have fun at the club." With a wave, her daughter vanished.

"Okay, toots," she told Ginger. "I know I'm young for a grandma, but I'd better give these muscles a pounding or I'm going to start to sag."

The baby cooed, happy to go along.

FRODO FLUNG himself at Jason the moment he walked in the door. Between playing with the eager creature and consuming the pizza he'd brought home, the next hour passed quickly.

He was glad to see a note from Alice Gray that she and her sons had visited Frodo after school and taken him out to play. Pets, like children, required care and affection. Even so, the pup had chewed up a couple of stray socks, a fact that made Jason wonder all over again why he'd been so eager to get it.

"Because you're cute," he told the little dog as he cuddled it.

Still, he had to admit that he'd never yielded to his desire for a puppy before. Something about the welcoming atmosphere of Serene Beach made him feel at home. And a home wasn't complete without someone to share it with.

For some reason, Heather's image came to him, the way she'd looked yesterday in that stunning reddish-brown dress. He didn't know what had inspired him to drape her with the scarf when he normally took zero interest in fashion.

The woman exuded sensuality, that was the point. He'd yearned to touch her, and the scarf had provided an excuse.

Jason leaned back on the couch and let his eyelids drift shut while Frodo played around his feet. He couldn't relax, though, not with visions of Heather floating through his mind.

The gown had fitted her like the proverbial glove, except that gloves weren't cut that low. They didn't have slits up the side, either. It was too bad Heather usually wore slacks or demure skirts, because she had great legs. If Jason could have found an excuse, he'd have loved to run his hands from her ankle all the way up to where the slit ended at her thigh.

He wanted to see her. Just to talk, of course. Being around her made him feel good.

One excuse was as good as another, Jason supposed, and went to snap a leash on Frodo. If he happened to be passing by while walking his pooch, what was wrong with stopping to say a friendly hello? The risk of being spotted by the manager was worth taking.

Half an hour later, he returned, having made his dog

happy but failed in his mission. No one had answered Heather's door and she wasn't in the pool, either.

Come to think of it, she'd mentioned a health club. As he released Frodo from the leash, Jason remembered seeing one nearby. He doubted he'd be lucky enough to corner her tonight, but he needed to get back into an exercise routine anyway, so he might as well check it out.

He drove the few blocks and parked in the adjacent lot. The place wasn't crowded at this early-evening hour, he discovered as he toured it, and, although modest in size, it had a full complement of facilities plus a coffee shop in the lobby. Its most significant attraction, however, was the sight of Heather pedaling on an exercise machine.

He'd guessed right! What a lucky break.

Jason withdrew before she glimpsed him. "Sign me up," he told the attendant. "I'm short on time. How long will this take?"

"Just a few minutes." The young woman smiled as he shifted edgily from foot to foot. "Why don't you go ahead and throw on your exercise clothes while I prepare the forms?"

"Done." Gear bag over one shoulder, Jason jogged to the locker room.

When he finished signing the papers and returned to the exercise room, there were three other occupants: a young couple talking earnestly as they strode side by side on twin treadmills, plus Heather, still cycling intently, lost in whatever she was listening to on earphones.

A gray crop top and matching shorts clung to her curves as she cycled furiously. Although the butterfly was out of sight, her slender waist begged to have two masculine hands encircle it.

Better to look elsewhere. At her straight, delicate shoulders, perhaps, or the short, mussed hair that ruffled like a wildfire in a breeze.

Jason took the machine next to hers and set to his task, stealing glances at her from time to time. Soon he felt the half painful, half pleasurable stretch of muscles at work and an even more enjoyable tug in his midsection.

Heather, who had taken no notice of him, nodded to herself as she listened to her CD player. Faintly, Jason heard a Latin rhythm.

He found it peaceful to be this close without arousing her usual antagonism. Too bad they'd gotten off on the wrong foot in Atlanta, although perhaps *foot* wasn't the right word, since apparently they'd done more lying down than standing.

He wished he knew how to recapture the mutual attraction they'd shared. If only he could fly back through time and do it all over again.

A shriek startled him from his reverie. Heather yanked off her earphones so fast they flew into the air. She snatched at them, missed, and had to grab again, barely catching them before they fell.

"Learning to juggle?" Jason teased. "You might want to start with something simpler than headphones."

"Jason Carmichael!" she roared. "What are you doing here?"

He gestured at the cycle. "Isn't it obvious? I'm working out."

"How long have you been next to me?"

"Five, ten minutes," he said. "What tape are you playing? I like the beat."

"You have no business getting close enough to hear my music!" She glared at him, her ample chest heaving. If only he could remember what that chest looked like without the crop top, Jason mused, more annoyed at his faulty memory than ever. "I don't like you invading my space in my spare time. Why don't you find another gym?"

"This place is convenient. I live right down the street," he pointed out.

"Please don't remind me!"

"Serene Beach is a small town," Jason said. "Didn't anyone warn you that you were likely to run into your colleagues away from Doctors Circle?"

"Not every evening!" she protested. "I've managed to retain my privacy just fine for three years, until you came along."

"I should think you'd want to extend a warm welcome to a lonely single male newly arrived in town." It was hard to keep from chuckling at her obvious indignation, but he managed.

Something about Heather brought out the teasing side of Jason. It had displayed itself only rarely in the past, mostly to give his exhausted fellow medical students a humor break. He was enjoying the experience.

"I don't belong to the neighborhood welcome club, or to a lonely hearts club, either," Heather retorted. "Look, I can't stop you from using this health club, but as mature adults we can both agree to avoid each other. Either we can come here on different schedules or we can choose different activities."

"No," he said.

"What do you mean, no?" She sounded on the verge of snarling, which reminded him of Edith's remark.

"Did you really growl at George the other day?" Jason asked.

"What?"

"Never mind." He decided to answer her previous question before she got so frustrated she pummeled him. "I find health clubs intrinsically boring."

"Then why join one?" Grumpily, she resumed pedaling. Jason took it as a sign of resignation.

"*A,* I like to keep in shape," he said. "We doctors ought to set a good example for the general public."

"What's *B?*"

"*B* is that while health clubs in general may be boring, I find this one very entertaining." The long sentence put a strain on his breathing. Exercising and conversation didn't mix well, but this was worth the effort.

"What's entertaining about it?" Heather asked.

"You're here."

She digested this information for a moment before saying, "You mean you plan to amuse yourself by irritating me?"

"I prefer to think of myself as enlivening an otherwise tedious situation." Jason didn't like to think about what Edith would say if she learned he was bedeviling Dr. Rourke again. But since when did he worry about what anyone else thought?

Heather frowned at him for a moment. Finally, she said, "Suit yourself." After clamping her earphones back into place, she resumed pedaling.

The young couple departed, slinging towels around their necks. Heather labored on, ignoring Jason. This was no longer any fun. Besides, Edith's comment about Heather taking leave had been bothering him. There would never be a better time to ferret out the truth.

Jason doubted Heather would confide in him of her own free will. A flanking tactic might work, however.

"Excuse me," he said.

With an impatient release of breath, Heather removed her earphones. "Yes?"

"I hate gossip, don't you?"

She nodded impatiently. "I despise it."

"Then you should remember that the best way to short-circuit gossip is to tell the truth," he said.

"I always tell the truth." She started to turn away.

"You don't always tell the whole truth," he challenged. "For example, you haven't explained why you took leave last fall."

Her forehead furrowed. "That's none of your business."

"Doctors Circle is abuzz with speculation. Why not put an end to it?"

Heather's gaze raked him icily. "A person is entitled to privacy. Besides, that's old news."

Darn, this wasn't working. He had to up the ante.

"Some people believe you were angry about my being hired." Jason watched her closely. He hoped this wasn't true, but if it were, they might as well get it into the open.

"Hogwash." Heather was so distressed, she didn't even resume cycling. "That is too much."

"What is?"

"You and your prying." She climbed off the exercise machine. "You're going to have to amuse yourself with somebody else, Doctor. I've had enough for one night."

Perhaps he *had* gone too far, Jason thought. Swinging down, he fell into place beside her. "I apologize."

Heather broke stride. She really was tiny, he thought.

At least, most of her was. "Does this mean you're going to leave me alone in the future?"

"I can't be accountable for my actions in the future," he said.

"Why not?"

"Call me a creature of impulse." The remark surprised Jason. Impulsive, him? Only with Heather.

"You're like Dr. Jekyll and Mr. Hyde," she said. "At the office, you're a bossy pain in the neck."

"But what am I at the health club?" Although he knew he was opening himself up for a major insult, it was worth it to find out what Heather might say.

"I refuse to comment." Leaving him unsatisfied, she marched out of the room.

Jason wanted to continue the conversation but he could hardly follow her into the ladies' locker room. Wondering what imp got into him whenever he was around the woman, he went to shower and change.

When he came out, Heather was easing the flame-haired baby into a stroller. "May I ask why you brought Ginger along?"

"Because my…" She gave a little cough. "My niece is tied up tonight."

"Tied up?" Jason had no interest in what Olive might be doing. He simply wanted to prolong the conversation.

"She went out with friends."

"I didn't realize mothers got a night off." He wished the young woman would materialize and take her baby. If Heather didn't have to care for this cute little tyke, she'd be more likely to respond to a heartrending appeal to come home and help him tame his sock-eating puppy.

"Shocking, isn't it?" Lips pursed, Heather adjusted a blanket around the infant. "Mothers are nothing more than pack animals, at least as far as some fathers are concerned. We should be happy laboring day and night until we keel over in the traces.''

"I was making conversation, not proposing to enslave the female half of the human race," Jason said.

She straightened. "Sorry. You pushed one of my buttons."

"I seem to be doing that a lot." Moving ahead of her, he held the door. "Did you walk here?"

"You're new to Southern California, aren't you?" she said.

"I don't see how that follows."

"If you'd grown up in the greater L.A. area, you'd know that no one thinks of walking, not even a few blocks to a health club." Heather chuckled at the irony.

Jason was glad she'd calmed after her earlier tirade. Whatever he'd said to set her off, apparently it hadn't been a serious offense. "You *are* from around here, I take it."

"Northridge." She pushed the stroller across the parking lot to a silver sedan with a child seat in the back. "That's on the other side of L.A."

Although he didn't understand why, Jason was reluctant to head for his own car, which he'd driven because he hadn't been certain of the distance to the health club. Being around Heather made him keenly aware of how lonely his town house was, in spite of Frodo.

"Let me take you out for ice cream," he said. "The kid's a little young but she might enjoy a lick."

"She's yawning." Heather finished strapping her in and slid behind the wheel. "Thanks for the offer, but I'll pass."

Jason had to let her go. "See you tomorrow."

"Sure thing." Heather started the engine. He watched

her glance over the seat back to check on the baby before putting the car in gear.

She certainly was a doting great-aunt. If Jason hadn't known better, he might have assumed that the baby was hers and Olive merely the hired nanny, taking her evening off.

Grumpy from being rejected, he steered his Mercedes to the ice cream parlor and bought a quart of rocky road to eat by himself. In the past, he'd rather enjoyed spending time alone. What on earth made him feel so grumpy about it now?

Chapter Eight

White and pink flowers overflowed the fairytale wedding chapel and perfumed the air. Seated beside Olive's devoted grandfather, Heather felt her eyes fill with tears. Across the aisle, John's mother sniffled into her handkerchief while his father's eyes grew suspiciously bright.

The young couple stood arm in arm, facing the minister. From the rear, Olive's satin gown flowed smoothly over her slim figure, while John stood tall in his uniform. As his fiancée had noted, his red hair was almost a match for Heather's.

Olive's friend Julia, the maid of honor, and John's brother as his best man completed the tableau. The small wedding, in this gemlike setting, gave Heather the sensation that they were all figures on a wedding cake, frozen in one perfect moment. She almost wished they really could stay here forever, enjoying this special occasion that crowned so many hopes and dreams.

When she was a little girl, she used to stage pretend weddings with her dolls. They were never luxurious enough to suit her. "When I get married, I'll have a church full of orchids," she recalled saying to her mother. "And so much white lace, we'll have to send to France for it."

Of course, there hadn't been a wedding. When she'd been a teenager, that loss had torn at her almost as if she'd lost a limb. Since then, as she'd become absorbed in her medical career, she'd almost forgotten her keen desire to walk down the aisle.

What if things had been different? Heather wondered. What if Ned had been man enough to take responsibility for his child?

Her life would certainly have turned out differently. Not necessarily for the best, she had to admit. The cost and long hours would have prevented her from becoming a doctor, and it was unlikely a marriage between two such immature people would have lasted. Most likely she'd have become a divorced single mother, struggling to make ends meet.

Her thoughts drifted to Jason. Resplendent in a tuxedo, he waited for her beneath a rose-covered trellis. With a jaunty smile playing across his face, he was so handsome she could hardly wait to run into his arms.

Heather blinked and dragged herself back to reality. Why on earth was she picturing Jason as a groom? He'd abandoned his fiancée and, in Atlanta, given Heather the cold shoulder after believing he'd slept with her. He was the last man on earth to rely on.

In Heather's lap, Ginger began to babble. Other people turned to smile at the baby. She was glad she had her family around her, most of all this precious grandchild.

It had been a long struggle since her teenage years, but since her one big mistake in trusting Ned, she'd made the right choices. Today, celebrating the future with her daughter and granddaughter was all the reward she could ask for.

After saying a firm "I do!" Olive hurried over, swept

up her daughter and carried her to the altar. John engulfed them both in a hug as he added his own vow.

Seeing the new family together tipped the scales, and tears slid openly down Heather's cheeks. She didn't bother to fumble for a tissue, since even Olive's grandpa was crying.

Afterward, they posed for photographs and gathered for a cake-and-champagne reception in the couple's bridal suite. While Olive retreated to the bedroom to change out of her long white gown, John assured Heather that she was welcome to visit them any time.

"You've meant a great deal to Olive these past few months. To me, too, knowing that you were there with her," John said. At close range, Heather could see that he had entrancing green eyes. No wonder her daughter had fallen for him!

"I'm overjoyed to be part of your lives," she said. "More than I can tell you."

"Hey, I'm honored to have you for a mother-in-law." He refilled her champagne glass. "When Olive told me she'd contacted you, I wasn't sure at first that it was such a good idea. But I'm glad it worked out."

"And we're thrilled that you can watch Ginger for the week," Olive added, joining them. A quick-change artist, she looked radiant in a pink cocktail dress. "After a few more days in Vegas, we're going to drive to Hoover Dam and to Arches National Park."

"I'm afraid camping would be kind of hard on a baby," John added.

"She'll be fine with me." Heather had arranged for Amy Ladd's Aunt Mary, who ran a home day-care center, to supervise Ginger during the weekdays. Amy herself had promised to take the baby during any evening or late-night deliveries.

"Quent and I have talked about having one of our own," Amy had explained. "Of course, Tara and Greg *are* our own, now that we're adopting them. Still, a baby would be so sweet. Although maybe I'll change my mind after Ginger wakes me up at all hours." She didn't sound as if she meant it.

After all, how could anyone resist a cutie like this? Heather thought, watching her granddaughter burble happily in her father's arms.

"We'll be fine, won't we?" she asked Ginger.

The response came in a string of high-pitched syllables. Heather didn't require an interpreter. She knew the answer was yes.

THE PHONE sounded in the depths of darkness. Jason, having long ago mastered the art of coming fully awake even from the deepest sleep, grabbed it on the third ring.

"Dr. Carmichael," he rasped.

"It's George Farajian. Sorry to wake you, Doctor." The obstetrician's voice had the overly bright tone of a man who's been awake too long. "Spring has sprung and the babies are arriving in droves. You did offer emergency backup, you'll recall."

Jason checked the clock. Two in the morning. He stifled a groan. "I'll be right there."

He swung off the bed and stepped on something soft. It let out a yip.

"Frodo! I'm sorry." He hoped the pup wasn't hurt, and also that it hadn't awakened a neighbor who might complain to the manager. "Poor baby."

Despite the need to soothe the puppy and to make himself presentable, Jason managed to arrive at Doctors Circle in half an hour. By contrast with the silent streets and empty courtyard, the first-floor Labor and Delivery area of the Birthing Center bustled with activity.

Dr. Farajian, who specialized in high-risk pregnancies, had taken the most difficult delivery for himself. Two other doctors were busy with more routine cases, while a Caesarian patient was being prepped for Jason.

Performing surgery was both a learned skill and an inherent ability. The delicate task had always fascinated Jason, whose painstaking care resulted in a low rate of complications. He was glad George had trusted him with the patient.

Despite the risk,. the procedure went smoothly. The little boy wailed lustily after emerging and weighed nearly five pounds despite being six weeks premature.

"That's a good sign," said the neonatologist, Dr. Quentin Ladd. "Hey, little fellow, let's check you out."

Jason finished sewing up the patient, a young woman whose husband had grown so pale during the first incision that one of the nurses had suggested he step outside. He'd recovered, however, and was regaling his wife with a description of every twitch their son made.

"He's got a great pitching arm," the father said. "Wouldn't you say, Dr. Ladd?"

"Absolutely. Your only problem will be deciding which major league team he should play for." Quent maintained a deadpan expression.

It was nearly 4:00 a.m. by the time Jason stripped off his gown, mask and gloves. "Any more deliveries?" he asked the charge nurse.

She shook her head. "They always wait until the doctors are sound asleep. You should know that."

"I hoped it was different in California," Jason joked.

"Want to grab some breakfast?" Quent asked.

"You bet." Since it was Sunday, he didn't have to

worry about trying to snatch a few hours of sleep before office hours. The cafeteria, located across the way, remained dark, Jason noticed. "What's the closest all-nighter?"

"The Coffee King," the young man said. "It's a block away. You can follow me from the parking garage."

"Will do."

A few minutes later, the two men took seats in a booth near a window. Set on a bluff, the coffee shop overlooked a broad section of Serene Beach.

Below and to Jason's right lay the beach area, mostly dark at this hour. To his left spread the harbor, where lights showed a sleepy array of yachts and sailboats.

"You don't happen to own a boat, do you?" Jason asked.

"No, but the Barrs do," Quent said. "Sooner or later, you'll be invited to a party on their yacht. It's a lot of fun."

"It sounds like it." From what Jason had heard, Patrick hosted several gatherings a year for the staff. He wasn't used to partying with his colleagues, although he could see how it would build morale. "Is that where he holds the famous Christmas reception I've heard so much about?"

"No, that's at his mansion," Quent said. "Sometimes he also loans out his cabin in the mountains as a prize in employee promotions, or so I hear. I've never been there." He explained that it was located at a mountain ski resort a two-hour drive from Serene Beach.

A cabin in the mountains. That would make a splendid getaway place, Jason thought, and wondered whether Heather liked to ski.

A waitress stopped to fill their coffee cups. After scanning the menu, Quent said, "I'll have the cholesterol special."

"That sounds good to me, too," Jason said.

The waitress didn't bat an eye at their unconventional terminology. She must get a lot of medical personnel as clients. "Two bacon-and-egg combos, coming up."

After she left, Quent showed him photos of the niece and nephew he and his wife Amy had adopted. The two of them had married in order to gain custody, the neon-atologist explained, but had quickly fallen in love as well.

"Now we're ready to have a new baby," he said. "The kids are excited, and Amy and I can't wait."

Jason had never allowed himself to dwell on the possibility of having kids. The new father's excitement this morning had been contagious, though. It would be fun to have a little boy to share ball games and romps with the dog. Or a girl, a cute one who looked like Heather. She might like ball games and romps with the dog, too.

"How did you know Amy was the right woman?" The whole subject of love baffled him. It seemed immensely complicated and full of room for error.

"I realized I wanted to spend the rest of my life with her," Quent said. "Wherever she is, I feel at home. It's that simple."

Was it? As far as Jason was concerned, his home was wherever he paid the rent.

Their orders arrived, along with coffee refills. Despite being a relative newcomer, Quent proved a fount of knowledge about people at Doctors Circle. It occurred to Jason that he might be able to answer the one question bothering him.

"Your wife is a good friend of Dr. Rourke's," he

said. "Did she mention why Heather took leave last fall?"

Quent made a wry face. "Sorry. I'm sworn to silence."

"You mean there's a deep dark secret?" It irked Jason that this fellow sitting across the table knew more about Heather than he did.

"I don't know if you'd call it that. It was personal, and Heather values her privacy," Quent said.

Jason swallowed the impulse to push harder. He supposed he had no right to snoop into Heather's private life. But what on earth could she be hiding?

The other doctor continued talking, distracting him with stories about other staff members at Doctor's Circle. The funniest one concerned Dr. Barr and his wife, Natalie, who was his longtime secretary.

They'd had a brief affair, then decided to let things cool off. Even after she got pregnant, it had taken Patrick a while to realize the baby belonged to him and not to Natalie's ex-husband, with whom he'd wrongly believed she was reconciled.

"So here was Patrick blissfully unaware that his secretary was carrying his baby while she got bigger and bigger right in front of him." Quent laughed at the memory.

"Why didn't she tell him?"

"I've never been clear about that," he admitted. "Some female thing, I guess."

"*Some female thing?* Is that a medical term?"

"Don't ask me," his companion parried. "I take care of the babies, not the mothers. You're the obstetrician."

"I never claimed to understand women," Jason said. "Not beyond the strictly medical sense."

"I guess not." Realizing his comment might be taken

as an insult, Quent said, "It's just that my wife tells me you and Heather rub each other the wrong way. I'm sure it's no big deal."

"We have misunderstandings every now and then. It's nothing that World War III couldn't settle."

As they paid the check and left, Jason reflected back over the conversation, especially the way Quent had clammed up about the subject of Heather's leave.

What kind of secret would make a woman disappear for two months without explanation? Could it be a health problem? If so, Jason wanted to help.

He wished Heather weren't out of town for the wedding. Maybe he should drop by her town house and sound out her niece, who probably knew the truth. At this time of the morning, though, he'd probably wake her up and set the baby to crying.

Jason was driving home, his subconscious mind churning full-tilt, when the pieces started fitting together. One fact in particular struck him: If his mental calculations were correct, Heather had taken leave about the time Ginger must have been born.

He'd noticed more than once that something seemed odd about the situation. Heather took considerably more interest in Ginger than he would have expected of a great-aunt. And the baby resembled her a lot more than it resembled Olive.

Patrick had had no idea Natalie was pregnant with his child, in spite of the fact that they'd made love. Was it possible that history was repeating itself at Doctors Circle?

At the gym, Jason had joked about not realizing mothers got nights off. He could almost swear that when Heather answered, she'd used the pronoun *we* in referring to mothers.

But Heather wasn't a mother. Or was she?

Jason gripped the steering wheel hard. He was struck again by the memory of kissing that butterfly on Heather's stomach. If they *had* made love, Ginger might be the result.

He halted the car in his garage. As he sat behind the wheel, his mind ran through the numbers just to make sure he wasn't going crazy.

They'd met in Atlanta about fifteen months ago. Ginger must be close to six months old. And Heather had gone on a two-month leave about four weeks before her birth.

He could hear his heart pounding in the silence. Was it possible he had a daughter?

Surely the staff at a maternity hospital would have noticed if one of the obstetricians were pregnant. Yet every woman carried her baby differently. With her large bust, the aid of a white coat and the complicity of her nurse, Heather might have pulled it off.

It must have been difficult. Jason wished he'd been there to help and to watch Ginger grow. He'd felt plenty of unborn babies move, listened to their heartbeats and examined them on sonograms. But his own daughter...

The scientific side of Jason's mind warned that he should take this slowly. There could be a flaw in his reasoning.

In his heart, though, he knew he was right. He had a child, and Heather was the mother. Maybe that's why he'd felt so strongly drawn to her since he arrived. That was why he found Ginger so bright and charming.

The time had come to talk to Heather. Sitting in his car, Jason rapid-dialed her number.

WHO COULD BE calling this early on her cell phone? Fortunately, Heather was already awake, happily feeding

Ginger a morning bottle as they both lounged in her queen-size hotel bed.

She fumbled the phone, one-handed, to her ear. "Dr. Rourke."

"It's Jason."

Well, of course. Who else would have the nerve? On the other hand, maybe he was calling about the medical center. "Does this concern one of my patients?"

"No," he said. "It's personal."

"Anything wrong at my town house?" Perhaps he'd seen someone trying to break in, Heather thought with a spurt of worry.

"It's about Atlanta."

Her first reaction was relief that nothing had gone wrong. It was replaced by grumpiness. Why was he dragging this up again, and at this hour? "Give me a break!" she sputtered. "What did you do, lie awake all night figuring out ways to pester me? It's six o'clock on Sunday morning!"

"I thought it was an hour later there."

"No, it isn't!"

"Sorry." Jason sounded apologetic, which mollified Heather slightly. "I was up early with a C-section."

"Did everything go all right?" Heather felt a flick of sympathy for the man, who must have had a tough night.

"Fine," he said.

"I'm sorry you lost sleep," Heather told him. "But getting called in for surgery doesn't give you the right to bother me on vacation."

"Did I wake you?" he asked.

"No." She decided not to offer an explanation of why she wasn't sleeping. Ginger, however, took the initiative by disengaging from the bottle and issuing a loud burp.

"What was that?" Jason said.

"What did it sound like?"

"It sounded like someone burped in the background."
He paused before saying, "Are you alone?"

"No, as a matter of fact, I'm not."

For one delicious instant, she figured she'd trumped
him with the presence of an imaginary male companion.
Then he said, "That didn't sound like a guy burp. That
sounded like a baby burp."

"That was a baby burp," she admitted. "I'm feeding
Ginger. Her mother's busy."

"Her mother seems to be busy frequently. Where's
her father?"

"None of your business." Why was he probing into
Olive's private life?

Heather supposed she could clear up her reason for
babysitting by explaining about the wedding and honeymoon without having to reveal that she was a grandmother instead of a great-aunt. Right now, however, she
was in no mood to satisfy Jason's idle curiosity.

"I think you owe me an explanation," said the in-
credibly presumptuous man at the other end of the call.

Was he out of his mind, or simply the victim of a
runaway ego? "I don't owe you anything," Heather
said. "You have a lot of nerve. First you move into my
town home development, then you join my health club,
now you call and demand information that doesn't concern you. What I do when I'm away from work is—"

"—none of my business," he concluded. "Listen, I
didn't mean to upset you. Can't we have a calm, rational
conversation like two adults?"

"This is a rational conversation," Heather said. "I
have never been more rational in my life. What I also
am, in case you hadn't noticed, is ticked off!"

With that, she punched End. It was the first time she ever recalled hanging up on a conversation.

Maybe it wasn't the most politic thing to do to her supervisor, Heather supposed. On the other hand, he was way out of line.

The man apparently enjoyed provoking her, like an adolescent with a crush, except that she didn't kid herself into thinking it was anything of the sort. She supposed she'd opened herself to this kind of nonsense when she got involved with Jason in the first place, but for heaven's sake, they weren't involved anymore.

She looked down at her granddaughter. "Baba?" Ginger said.

Heather's irritation melted. "You're the sweetest little thing in the world."

"Da," came the cheerful response.

"I suppose his attention is kind of flattering," Heather told the infant. "Lots of people think Jason is gorgeous. Okay, he *is* gorgeous. He's just not my type."

The baby reached for her bottle. Heather angled her into a more comfortable position.

"I don't have a type," she added, for good measure. "But if I did, Jason Carmichael wouldn't be it."

She was certain Ginger agreed.

CALLING HEATHER at such an early hour hadn't been a good idea, Jason conceded as he got out of the car. Although the thought made him want to pound his fist into the dashboard, he should have considered the possibility that she might be in bed with another man.

Thank goodness she wasn't. Nevertheless, hearing that she was giving Ginger her morning feeding confirmed his suspicions. He'd never heard of a great-aunt getting that involved with an infant.

A father! The possibility was exhilarating. Jason barely restrained himself from skipping along the walkway like a boy.

Confronting Heather had backfired, however. Not only hadn't she opened up to him, she'd performed the digital-age version of slamming down the phone.

What they needed was time alone away from the job. If they could unwind gradually, she might admit of her own accord that they had been lovers, and that Jason was Ginger's father.

Quent's mention of a cabin in the mountains gave Jason an idea. More than an idea: He already had the beginnings of a plan.

Chapter Nine

Heather came to work early on Monday to check on the progress of her nurse's pregnancy. Cynthia had insisted on being treated by her and no one else, and it suited them both to conduct the examination away from the pressure of regular hours.

"It looks as if you may be able to carry to term, which is a blessing with twins," Heather said after she finished. "However, you must be uncomfortable standing on your feet all day. The center offers generous maternity leave. Although I'd really miss your help, you should take advantage of it."

Cynthia's dark hair swung from side to side, registering a negative. "I'm saving as much time as possible to spend with them after they're born."

"Get dressed and let's talk in my office."

The young woman checked her watch. "It's getting late."

"We'll be fine."

A few minutes later, Cynthia joined her. Although the office was small, Heather chose a chair beside her nurse rather than putting a desk between them. "Let's talk about how we're going to handle things. For one, we'll rearrange your schedule after you give birth. You'll need flexibility.''

"Please, no special privileges for me," Cynthia said. "I got myself into this mess and I can handle it."

The mess involved her ex-boyfriend, who had turned out not only to be married but to have three children. He and his wife, whom he'd kept in the dark, were moving to Alaska. He'd promised to send money, but how likely was a liar and a cheat to keep his word?

"I'll be glad to help in any way I can." With Olive gone on her honeymoon, Heather was learning firsthand how hard it was to care for a child alone.

That morning, she'd awakened an hour early to feed and dress Ginger, and still had barely managed to arrive at the day-care home on schedule. The very idea of supervising twins made her heart go out to the young woman.

Uneasily, she recalled what Jason had said about their patients deserving the best. He wasn't going to tolerate frequent absences by her nurse, and she had to admit she could see his point of view.

"I know it's going to be complicated, but that's my problem, not yours," Cynthia said.

"Kids get sick and caretakers can be unreliable," Heather said. "If it helps, we can transfer you to a position where it won't matter so much if you're late. Don't worry, I'll make sure there's no decrease in salary."

Cynthia's eyes misted. "Please don't do that! I love working with you."

"I feel the same way," Heather admitted. "It's the new clinic I'm worried about. Dr. Carmichael has exacting standards. I'm not sure you've fully come to terms with what it's going to mean, being the parent of twins."

"I'll discuss it with Mrs. Ladd." Cynthia was in counseling with Amy. "Please don't make any changes until I talk to her."

"Don't worry, I won't. My main concern is for you," Heather said. *And I wish I could give that jerk of an ex-boyfriend a piece of my mind.*

At times like this, she was tempted to think ill of the entire masculine gender, until she pictured her son-in-law in uniform, his face suffused with joy as he escorted Olive up the aisle. What a terrific man!

She recalled her mental image of Jason as a groom. Would he ever be ready to devote himself to a woman and a home? Not likely, when he couldn't even bear the thought of planting flowers!

Cynthia tapped her watch. "I can't take up any more of your time."

"Yes, you can. But not necessarily right now," Heather agreed.

A full complement of patients kept her so busy she didn't come up for air until midday. Coral, who always seemed to appear around noon, stopped by to ask if she could spare a few minutes to talk to Dr. Carmichael.

"He wants to do some planning." The secretary wore her usual anxious expression. "That's all he told me."

"Sure, I can come." She might as well be accommodating, Heather decided. Keeping the department head in a good mood was in everyone's best interest.

Maybe if he saw plenty of her at the office, he'd be less inclined to haunt her health club and wake her up with phone calls. She wouldn't bet on it, though.

Relief showed on Coral's face. "That would be great."

They crossed the courtyard beneath a lowering sky.

When Heather entered Jason's office, he clicked off his computer. "Thanks for coming."

"What's going on?" she asked. "I heard you're doing some kind of planning."

Before replying, he studied her as if she had data digitally encoded in her freckles. Meeting his gaze frankly, Heather took a chair.

There was something different about him today, she thought. There was a gentler light in his green eyes, an easier line to his jaw. He must be pleased with the way the clinic was taking shape.

"I'm planning a retreat for the new doctors." Jason came around and sat on the front of his desk. "It'll be an opportunity for all of us to get to know each other away from the office, to share ideas and make sure we're on the same wavelength."

"A retreat?" Although she hadn't expected this, Heather didn't object. She was a bit intimidated about working with such prominent individuals as Alexei Davidoff and Lisa Arcadian. Getting together outside work should help meld them into a more effective team.

"I've arranged to borrow Dr. Barr's cabin in the mountains. It will give us privacy, and we can throw in some skiing, too," Jason said.

Although he wasn't touching her, she felt the heat of his skin and became acutely aware of the rise and fall of his chest. Thank goodness when he said *privacy,* he meant for the whole group, not just the two of them.

"I don't ski. But the others might enjoy it," she said. "When did you have in mind?"

"Next weekend," Jason said.

Heather nearly groaned aloud. Ginger would still be staying with her. "I can't."

"Why not?"

"I'll still be taking care of my great-niece." Before he could point out that that was Olive's responsibility, she added, "Her mother's already left on a trip and won't be back till Monday."

"Bring the baby along." Jason made it sound as if carting a baby to a conference, however informal, were the most natural thing in the world.

"You're kidding." Heather wrinkled her nose. "Alexei and Lisa will think I'm a flake."

"We're in the business of making babies," Jason said. "I don't see how it can hurt to have one around."

Neither of the other doctors was a parent, as far as Heather knew. They weren't likely to enjoy cries in the night or messes in the morning. "Let's pick another date."

"With everyone moving in, we'll be overwhelmed getting ready to open in April," he said. "It's the only weekend that works for everybody."

About to point out tartly that it didn't work for her, Heather remembered her resolution not to cross Jason unnecessarily. It wasn't as if Olive, who checked in regularly on Heather's cell phone, was likely to have any objections. Better to save her arguments for something important, like securing concessions for Cynthia. "You're sure you don't mind? Even a sweet child like Ginger can be demanding. You might find her presence irritating."

"What kind of man would…" He stopped in midsentence, a muscle jumping in his jaw.

"Do your teeth hurt?" Heather asked.

"Do my what?" He stared at her as if she'd just parachuted from a space ship.

"You grimaced as if your teeth hurt. I know a good

dentist if you need one.'' She didn't mean to insult him. ''I'm sorry. Go ahead with what you were saying.''

Unaccustomed confusion showed on Jason's face. ''I lost my train of thought.''

''I was warning you that babies can interfere with other plans,'' Heather said.

''Oh, yes.'' He grinned. ''Has she ever seen snow?''

''Ginger? No.''

''You should buy her a snow suit so she can play in it,'' Jason said.

''She can't even stand up yet,'' Heather pointed out. ''She'd flop facedown in a drift. Maybe I could hold her on my lap and let her poke at it a little.''

''I'll help you.'' His eagerness startled her. ''I mean, when you want to take a break, I can play with the baby. It's only fair, since I'm the one dragging you away from your routine.''

Jason had never, ever, struck Heather as the kind of guy who liked to play with babies. As she recalled, he'd barely glanced at Ginger during their encounter at the health club. ''Is this some new wrinkle in employee relations?''

''What? Oh, yes, in a way,'' he said. ''I know I can be abrupt sometimes.''

''And you hope to improve your reputation by baby-sitting my great-niece?''

''Consider it part of honing my people skills.''

Heather overcame the temptation to point out that Jason's people skills needed more honing than he could accomplish in a single weekend. Or possibly a single lifetime. ''If you say so.''

''I'd be happy to give you a ride,'' he said. ''In case you don't like driving in the mountains.''

''I'll bring my own car, thank you.'' Heather didn't

intend to get stuck up there with no means of escape. She wasn't counting on Jason's goodwill toward Ginger outlasting one meal with baby food lobbed onto the front of his suit, or whatever he planned to wear.

Maybe a ski sweater. She could definitely picture him in tight-fitting jeans, or a snug T-shirt and shorts in the heat from the fireplace. She imagined his lazy smile welcoming her as she settled beside him.

She also imagined it mutating into a scowl as Ginger reached from her lap to poke an exploratory finger into his ear.

"Fine," Jason said. "You can leave work early on Friday if you'd prefer to arrive before dark." He handed her a computerized map with the address and directions.

"I'll be there." As she got to her feet, another thought occurred to her. "Is Eric Wong coming, too?" Although the embryologist had a Ph.D. rather than an M.D., he was one of the most important players in the department.

"I'm afraid he already had plans." Jason walked her to the door as if she were a guest. "I'm glad you can make it. I think this retreat will be beneficial for everyone."

"I'm sure it will." She wished she felt as positive as she sounded, Heather reflected as she walked back to the Ob/Gyn Department.

Alexei and Lisa weren't going to be seeing her at her most professional. She wouldn't get a chance to wear either of her new dresses, either, at such a casual retreat.

Still, it might work out well. If they proved friendly, she supposed it might be as good a time as any to explain her true relationship to Ginger.

When Olive had first contacted her, it had brought half-forgotten memories searing to the foreground, including the insults and snubs of her peers. Heather

GET FREE BOOKS and a FREE GIFT WHEN YOU PLAY THE...

SLOT MACHINE GAME!

Just scratch off the silver box with a coin. Then check below to see the gifts you get!

YES! I have scratched off the silver box. Please send me
the 2 free Harlequin American Romance® books and gift for which
I qualify. I understand I am under no obligation to purchase any books,
as explained on the back of this card.

354 HDL DRRM   **154 HDL DRR3**

FIRST NAME	LAST NAME

ADDRESS

APT.#	CITY

STATE/PROV.	ZIP/POSTAL CODE

7	7	7	Worth TWO FREE BOOKS plus a BONUS Mystery Gift!
🍒	🍒	🍒	Worth TWO FREE BOOKS!
♣	♣	♣	Worth ONE FREE BOOK!
🔔	🔔	🍒	TRY AGAIN!

Visit us online at www.eHarlequin.com

(H-AR-02/03)

DETACH AND MAIL CARD TODAY!

The Harlequin Reader Service® — Here's how it works:

Accepting your 2 free books and gift places you under no obligation to buy anything. You may keep the books and gift and return the shipping statement marked "cancel." If you do not cancel, about a month later we'll send you 4 additional books and bill you just $3.99 each in the U.S., or $4.74 each in Canada, plus 25¢ shipping & handling per book and applicable taxes if any.* That's the complete price and — compared to cover prices of $4.75 each in the U.S. and $5.75 each in Canada — it's quite a bargain! You may cancel at any time, but if you choose to continue, every month we'll send you 4 more books, which you may either purchase at the discount price or return to us and cancel your subscription.

*Terms and prices subject to change without notice. Sales tax applicable in N.Y. Canadian residents will be charged applicable provincial taxes and GST. Credit or debit balances in a customer's account(s) may be offset by any other outstanding balance owed by or to the customer.

hadn't been ready to let the gossips at Doctors Circle know about her painful past, or to deal with insensitive comments such as the one Jason had made about her nurse.

During the past few months, however, she'd grown more comfortable with the situation and discovered that she'd developed enough inner strength to handle whatever came up. In addition, she looked forward to leveling with Cynthia about the fact that she herself had been in a similar situation.

This weekend might prove to be a watershed in many ways, Heather supposed. At least, with Alexei and Lisa around, she didn't have to worry about any too-close-for-comfort encounters with Jason.

She was in the elevator en route to the second floor of her building when she remembered him saying that next weekend was the only one that worked for everyone. What about Eric Wong? It obviously didn't work for him.

When the doors opened, a receptionist signaled her urgently. ''Dr. Rourke! They need you in Labor and Delivery, right away!'' One of her patients was having an unexpectedly fast labor.

''I'm on my way,'' Heather said, and completely forgot whatever had been on her mind a moment earlier.

JASON WISHED he'd figured out a more convincing story to explain Eric's absence. He hadn't done badly, however, considering he'd had to improvise on the spot.

Alexei and Lisa would be arriving the following week, so neither of them was likely to give the game away in advance. He knew Heather would eventually see through his claim that they'd both cancelled at the last minute, but he hoped by then she would understand and perhaps even approve of his strategy.

His motives were pure. His tactics, he supposed, might be questionable. He'd also been purposely vague to Patrick when he arranged to borrow the cabin.

Jason experienced a twinge of anxiety, or perhaps it was guilt. He'd always done his best to play by the rules until now.

Yet if Heather hadn't deceived him, he wouldn't be in this position. And what was the alternative, insisting on a paternity test and trying to force her into letting him be a father to his daughter? It was much better to use gentle persuasion. Patrick, of all people, should understand when the truth came out.

It might be a good idea to get his story straight with the embryologist to prevent any crossed signals, Jason decided, and went down the hall to the lab. There he found Eric posing, somewhat uncomfortably, while Loretta snapped photos of him and his equipment.

She called a series of instructions that kept Eric shifting around for a series of shots. In her role as public relations director, there was no sign about her of the concerned infertility patient.

Her hormone treatments had begun the previous week. With luck, she might have healthy embryos ready to implant next month.

Eric spotted Jason. To Loretta, he said, "Don't you want to take some shots of Dr. Carmichael? He's more important than I am."

"What I'd prefer is both of you together." Loretta waved him into the scene. "One of you, pick up that petri dish and show it to the other one."

"We do that all the time," Jason joked as he followed

her directions. "We're always handing these things to each other."

"They make good Frisbees, except that they tend to break," Eric said, getting into the spirit.

Behind Loretta appeared a huge bouquet of orange-and-purple birds of paradise, white and yellow calla lilies and a sprinkling of smaller flowers. "Excuse me, Loretta, can I come through here?" asked a woman's dry voice.

The PR director glanced around. "Noreen! Those are perfect! Would you position them behind Dr. Carmichael and Dr. Wong?"

"Certainly." The bearer of the flowers turned out to be a sharp-faced woman in her seventies wearing a red-and-white volunteer's uniform. She plunked the bouquet onto the counter where the petri dish had been sitting before Jason picked it up. "There you go." She stuck out her hand. "I'm Noreen McLanahan. I met you at the reception after your press conference."

Her name rang a bell. She was, Jason recalled, a major supporter of Doctors Circle and a member of its board of directors as well as a volunteer. "It's good to see you again. Who sent the flowers?"

"They're from Dr. and Mrs. Barr to welcome Dr. Wong on board." Noreen scooted out of the frame and Loretta resumed taking photos.

"It's a nice gesture." Jason had appreciated the large bouquet he'd found on his desk soon after he arrived, as well.

"They're beautiful." The embryologist fingered one of the slender birds of paradise. "They make me feel at home. I'm originally from Hawaii."

"By way of Boston." Jason had worked with Eric

during his residency, and been so impressed that he'd recruited him for this job.

"Since you're standing around anyway," Noreen said from the sidelines, "I'd like to get your professional opinion on something, Dr. Carmichael."

"Go right ahead." He did his best to maintain a dignified, pleasant expression for the camera and hoped it didn't look as artificial as it felt.

"While my husband was alive, we were never able to have children. Things like you're doing now weren't available," Noreen said.

"The changes in the past twenty years have been amazing," Jason conceded.

"Now I find myself in the position of having a new boyfriend," the elderly woman continued. "I've been reading that women can give birth even after they've gone through menopause. Since I still have my original equipment, what are my chances, doc?"

Although Jason didn't think she was serious, he couldn't be sure. "How old are you?"

"Seventy-three," Noreen announced proudly. "I was thinking, we could make history. Not to mention racking up some splendid publicity for Doctors Circle if I got pregnant at my age, wouldn't you say, Loretta?"

The PR director made a choking noise before rallying. "We'd make the *National Enquirer,* at least."

"You'd need an egg donor," Eric added, joining the conversation.

"And a lot of hormones," Jason pointed out. Since he assumed she was joking, he decided not to mention that infertility clinics rarely agreed to treat a woman over fifty.

"I like hormones," Noreen said. "They make me feel

young again. Do you suppose I could dance the tango? If I took enough of them, I mean?''

"Before or after you got pregnant?" he asked.

She chuckled. "On second thought, I'm not so keen on this business of getting knocked up at the doctor's office. The old-fashioned way was much more fun."

"There's no age limit on that one, either." Loretta lowered her camera. "I think I've got enough, gentlemen. Thank you."

"I made them smile for you," Noreen said.

"You're a treasure." The younger woman put one arm around her. "What would we do without you?"

"Die of boredom," said Noreen. The two women exited together.

"She's adorable," Eric said. "She reminds me of my grandmother."

"You must have some grandmother." Jason stuck the petri dish on the counter.

"She can still perform a mean hula," he said.

"That I'd like to see." On the point of leaving, Jason recalled his purpose in seeking out Eric. "By the way, if anyone asks, you're busy next weekend."

"I am?"

"Go fishing or something," he said. "Just stay away from the mountains."

"The weather service is predicting snow and I love skiing." Eric had adopted the sport with a vengeance when he lived in Boston. "Seriously, I was thinking of heading up there. Once we start treating patients, it'll be hard to get away."

That might be all right if he went to a different area in the mountains. Unless, of course, he showed up on Monday with his leg in a cast and regaled Heather with the story of his skiing mishap.

"You're in Southern California. You should take up boating," Jason said.

"I get seasick."

"Then try sunbathing."

"What's going on?" Eric had never lacked curiosity, or forthrightness.

"I have some personal business to attend to with a certain lady," Jason said.

"Anyone I know?"

"Heather Rourke." That was as much as he cared to confide. "I'm arranging a retreat and the other staff members have been mysteriously called away. You had prior plans. And if you repeat this conversation to anyone…"

"I won't," Eric said. "I may need a return favor someday."

"Sounds good to me." Jason left while he was ahead. Matters were coming together so neatly, he would have believed this weekend was destined to succeed, if he'd been the kind of person who believed in destiny.

ONE PLAYPEN, check.

One portable high chair, check.

One diaper bag and a supply of diapers, check.

A stroller, baby wipes, bottles, formula, jars of baby food, bibs, booties, receiving cloths and umpteen changes of clothing for Ginger.

What had she forgotten?

"My suitcase," Heather said aloud. She unstrapped the baby from the car seat and carried her out of the garage and around the row of town houses. Bright overhead lights kept the early-evening darkness at bay.

It was hard to imagine how a grown woman could forget her own suitcase, until one saw how much stuff a baby required for a weekend, she thought as she fetched the overlooked valise. Balancing Ginger against her shoulder, she was on her way back to the car when Jason appeared.

In contrast to her own slightly disheveled state, he might have strolled from a resort ad. Sporty and suave in casual slacks and an open-collared shirt, he had a coat slung over one arm, an expensive leather case in one hand and a laptop carrier in the other. The man *would* bring his computer to a retreat.

"Where are your skis?" she asked.

"I'll rent some." His eyes flew to Ginger. "Is she dressed warmly enough?"

"I bought a coat for her." Although her granddaughter was unlikely to need it often, it did get cold in Texas. Besides, Heather didn't mind the expense. It was a lot more fun buying clothes for the baby than for herself.

"I'm afraid I've got a slight problem," Jason said.

"I hope you're not planning to bring your dog!"

He blinked a couple of times. "No, he's paying a visit to his former owners."

"Then what…" Heather could guess. None too happily, she said, "Your car?"

"It's making a funny noise." Jason assumed an expression of innocence that Heather didn't quite buy. "Normally, I'd take my chances, but I'd hate to get stranded in the mountains."

"How are Alexei and Lisa getting there?" Although the two new doctors hadn't showed up at Doctors Circle yet, Heather assumed they must have arrived in the area. "Maybe one of them could give you a ride."

"I don't know," Jason said. "Look, I can see that this is awkward. I'll go rent a car."

That, Heather concluded reluctantly, was an obvious

waste of money, since they lived in the same complex and were going to the same destination. "It'll make you at least an hour late."

"I'm sure you and our two new doctors will find plenty to talk about until I get there," he said blandly.

Heather gave an inward shudder at the prospect of making polite chitchat with two rather intimidating strangers while they waited for Jason.

"Forget it. You can ride with me."

"Thanks." To give him credit, he didn't gloat over his success, at least not where she could see it.

When they reached the car, he stowed their cases in the trunk while she strapped Ginger into her seat. The man deserved a comeuppance for presuming on her, Heather mused as she finished the task. Besides, as long as Jason was encroaching on her hospitality, he might as well make himself useful.

"Whoa!" she said when he started to get into the front passenger seat. "I'd prefer that you ride in the back. That way you can watch Ginger so I won't have to pull over to check if she starts to fuss."

She steeled herself for his protest. Instead, Jason's face lit up. "Great!"

"Why?" she asked.

"Why what?" He moved to the rear door.

"Why aren't you giving me an argument?"

"Because I don't want to," he said, and got in next to the baby.

Perhaps this wouldn't be such a difficult weekend after all, Heather reflected. With Jason on his best behavior, it might actually be fun.

She was almost looking forward to it.

Chapter Ten

In the dim light, Jason gazed into two inquisitive green eyes. If he'd had any remaining doubts about Ginger's parentage, her eye color—a match for his own—banished them.

"Hi," he said.

"Ba ba ba," said his daughter.

Alert and curious, she had pixielike features and perfectly formed little hands. A man could build a happy life with a child like this, taking her to the park, reading to her at night, holding her up to play with the ornaments on the Christmas tree.

It almost made Jason angry that Heather had tried to deny him these experiences. He had to acknowledge, however, that she had justification. In the grip of a hangover, he'd snarled that he didn't want to hear any more about what had happened between them, and she'd taken him at his word.

It must have been a shock to discover that she was carrying his baby, especially since they'd apparently tried to use contraception. He hated to think what she'd endured, going through the pregnancy alone, hiding it from her coworkers. And matters weren't necessarily easier now.

Jason had sometimes become impatient with colleagues who changed their schedules or left early because of day-care problems. Now he wondered how Heather managed. Obviously, she'd hired a nanny, but Olive seemed to feel entitled to take off an evening or an entire week whenever it suited her.

He almost said something right then. What was the point of continuing with this charade?

What stopped him was the probability that Heather would turn the car around and go home. Also, although she might be forced to acknowledge the truth, that didn't mean she would agree to share Ginger with him.

A nasty court battle wasn't in anyone's best interest, especially not his daughter's. It would be far, far better to improve their relationship to the point where Heather felt comfortable confiding in him and inviting him into her life.

Jason wasn't sure what that was going to entail. Until last Sunday, he'd had no intention of starting a family or of making a commitment of any kind beyond acquiring a puppy. Even then, he'd made sure he had a backup caretaker.

The more he thought about his daughter, though, the more he wanted to be with her every day. That didn't mean he was ready to get married, buy a house and plant roses. On the other hand, if they had their own house, Ginger could grow up with plenty of space and he wouldn't have to sneak Frodo out for walks.

A house? Tension knotted in Jason's throat. Taking on commitments meant limiting his future. It meant becoming like the many scientists he'd seen whose early promise dissipated after they settled down, sacrificing both their mobility and their edge.

He refused to worry about the future right now. The

important thing was to focus on his goal: ingratiating himself with Heather and getting to know their daughter.

To distract himself and amuse the fidgeting baby, Jason pointed at a school they were passing. On the illuminated athletic field, a group of kids played a lively game of soccer. "School," he told the baby.

"Ba ba?"

"Someday you might go to kindergarten there," he told her.

"La!" she said approvingly.

"I don't think she's smart enough to go to school there at five," came the unexpected remark from the front seat.

He bristled. "The heck she isn't!"

Heather's red hair shook from side to side. "Goodness, you've certainly taken a shine to her. I didn't peg you as the fatherly type."

You'd be surprised. Or rather, you will *be surprised.* "There's no reason Ginger can't go to kindergarten at that school, or anywhere she wants to."

"Yes, there is." They turned onto a thoroughfare leading toward the freeway. "It's a middle school. Didn't you take a look at the students?"

Although he supposed the children he'd seen might be a bit old for elementary school, Jason hated to admit defeat. "That doesn't prove anything. Maybe the school loans out its athletic field to older kids."

"It's a middle school," Heather repeated.

Grumpily, Jason asked, "What makes you the big expert?"

"I gave a talk there for the Moms in Training program on pregnancy prevention," she said.

You must have had fun explaining how you landed in the same predicament. Jason clamped his teeth together

to stifle the words. One remark like that and Heather
would put him out on the pavement. He'd deserve it,
too.

He remembered how she'd reacted to his remark that
her nurse should have used birth control. Jason winced
at the memory of his tactlessness. Too bad he hadn't
known then what he knew now, including the fact that
he was as susceptible to unbridled passion as anyone.

As he watched Ginger explore a cloth book with rapt
interest, he marveled at the miracle that had been created
by accident. How could he wish that anything had happened differently when it might have deprived them of
this child?

Thank goodness he and Heather were adults, capable
of supporting and caring for a child responsibly. The
issues were much more complicated for teenagers like
the ones she counseled.

A face appeared in his mind. Daniel, a buddy from
high school. Jason had run into him a few years ago at
their fifteenth reunion.

Back in high school, Daniel had gotten a girl pregnant.
Angry and confused, he'd refused to have anything to
do with her or their child.

At the reunion, Jason had learned the rest of the story.
After college and a childless marriage that ended in divorce, Daniel had sought out his son. He'd discovered
that the boy, adopted by a loving stepfather, had no interest in his birth father.

"He's probably the only child I'll ever have, and he
doesn't want anything to do with me," Daniel had said
in a voice ragged with regret. "I wish I'd had a crystal
ball when I was young so I could see the future. I'd have
done things a lot differently."

Jason didn't intend to make the same mistake. He was going to make sure Ginger grew up with a loving father.

DARKNESS HAD settled over the mountains by the time Heather parked in front of the A-frame cabin. Through the windshield, she gazed at a turbulent, starless sky.

"You don't think it's going to snow, do you? I forgot to check the weather report." There were no other cars in the driveway or along the curb, she noticed. "I hope Alexei and Lisa won't run into problems."

"Let's get inside and worry about them later." Jason opened his door. "Do you want me to unstrap Ginger?"

He and the baby had gotten along amazingly well on the journey. In the rearview mirror, Heather had glimpsed Jason trying to teach Ginger how to play patty-cake, although he didn't appear to grasp the principles very well himself. Later, he'd read to her in a rich voice that made *Spot the Dog* sound like a literary masterpiece.

When Heather stopped at a grocery store, he'd volunteered to stay in the car, although he'd insisted on providing money for food. It was a business expense, he'd pointed out. Thanks to the generous amount, Heather had loaded up on steaks, salmon and plenty of other items.

"I'd like to set up the playpen first so we have a safe place to put her inside while we unload." Although so far Ginger wasn't very mobile, Heather knew that a baby could start crawling without warning.

"It's best to be cautious," Jason agreed.

A few snowflakes swirled against Heather's nose as she got out of the car, and the chill wind reminded her to retrieve her coat. "What time are you expecting the others?" she asked.

"Any minute now." Jason went to unlock the front door before returning for the playpen.

They worked smoothly together, transferring the baby and their possessions indoors. Despite his strength, Jason moved with cautious gentleness. The way he held doors and insisted on carrying heavy items gave Heather an unfamiliar sense of being protected.

If he nudged against her more often than might be necessary, it only made her increasingly aware of his tangy aftershave lotion, which she didn't recall him wearing at work. The scent brought back tantalizing memories of Atlanta.

Heather dragged her attention away from Jason and set to figuring out the sleeping arrangements. Downstairs, the cabin provided two bedrooms. An open staircase led to a large loft equipped with a skylight and furnished as a master bedroom. It didn't require much math to figure that someone was going to have to sleep in the living room.

"I'll take the couch," she told Jason, who was bringing in firewood. "Ginger wakes up early. That way I can fix her breakfast without bothering anyone."

"We'll see," was his reply.

"It makes sense." Heather wanted a decision so she could figure out where to stow the rest of her gear before their colleagues arrived.

"Let's find out what the others have to say." Apparently the subject was closed. After a moment of internal debate, Heather decided not to make an issue of something so minor.

Jason knelt, layering the firewood and interspersing it with tinder. "I haven't done this for a long time."

"At least in Boston it made sense to build fires, unlike where I grew up." Heather lowered her granddaughter to a fluffy rug. "Most Southern California houses come with fireplaces, but you have to turn on the air conditioner to enjoy them."

"That sounds like fun," Jason said.

"It sounds like a waste of energy." Heather and her mother had battled with her father and brother on that point, and lost. "It must be a guy thing."

"What must?"

"Building fires," she said.

Kneeling by the hearth, he swung around to regard her with amusement. "Are you implying that I'm fulfilling some kind of primeval mandate?"

"I would never describe you as a caveman." As soon as the words were out, Heather remembered that she *had* once thought of him as a Neanderthal. Today, however, his behavior was not only civilized but charming.

"Never?" he teased.

"Rarely," she amended. Outside, the wind rose. "Did you hear a forecast?"

"I'm afraid not." Jason clicked on the TV and found the news.

Ginger paid no attention. She flopped onto her stomach, absorbed in the business of creeping.

"Doesn't that hurt her?" Jason asked as the little girl, after making a valiant effort to crawl, pitched forward onto her nose.

"Sometimes." Heather restrained her impulse to comfort the fussing child. Smothering an infant wasn't healthy. Sure enough, Ginger soon tired of whimpering and resumed her struggles.

"That rug might not be terribly clean," he said.

"It's good for kids to be around dirt." She'd read several articles on this point. "Some experts believe that children who don't get exposed to normal household germs at an early age are more vulnerable to allergies.''

"I'd like to review their data," Jason grumbled. "I'll bet they fudged it."

On the screen, an announcer said, "Now for the local weather. We're expecting three to four inches of snow tonight, folks. The sky should clear tomorrow, so get ready to hit the ski slopes."

"Perfect!" Jason said. "I much prefer natural snow to the artificial kind."

"What do you mean, it's perfect?" Heather demanded. "Alexei and Lisa still aren't here. You should be concerned about their safety!"

"Of course I am." Jason didn't sound very convincing.

Heather wasn't sure how, but she knew he was hiding something. "What's going on? Is there some kind of delay?"

"You might say that." He hesitated.

"Well?" she demanded.

Jason clicked off the TV. "I know I should have told you sooner. Alexei called to say he'd missed his flight, and Lisa…"

"When will they get here?"

He cleared his throat in the guiltiest manner Heather had ever witnessed. "That's a matter of interpretation."

"Don't tell me they're not coming!"

He ducked his head. It was as good as a confession.

"When did you find out?" she demanded.

"Just, uh…" His gaze fixed on Ginger. "She's eating something. What's she eating?"

Torn between concern for her granddaughter and frustration with Jason, Heather crooked her finger and swept it through the baby's mouth. Out came a small thread the color of her sleeper. "Nothing that will hurt her. Now tell me about Alexei and Lisa. How long have you known they weren't going to make it?"

He turned on the built-in gas jet in the fireplace. Flames leaped, igniting the kindling. "They weren't ever coming."

"What?"

"I apologize." The man quirked a grin at her. "You and I got off to a rough start, and this struck me as an opportunity to smooth out our differences."

"You set me up?" Heather couldn't believe his nerve. "You manipulated me into coming to the mountains alone with you?"

"More or less." Catching her glare, Jason added, "Think of it this way. We both get a weekend's vacation and we don't need to spend any more time together than seems comfortable. Ginger can have her own room and so can you."

"We have our own rooms at home." If she hadn't been so tired from the long drive and if the fire hadn't looked so inviting, Heather would have headed for the car immediately. Darn the man!

"At home, we'd never have taken the time to develop a good working relationship." Jason fixed the fire screen in place.

"And that's all you have in mind?"

"Absolutely."

"We already live practically next door," Heather said. "You didn't have to stage this craziness."

"We live halfway across the complex from each other," he corrected.

"You joined my health club."

"We've only run into each other once."

"On your first visit!" The man was outrageous. Cute,

too, but Heather was in no mood to be charitable. "Did Patrick know you tricked me into coming here?"

A tinge of red stained his cheeks. "No."

"You told him the same cock-and-bull story about a retreat?"

"I fudged." Jason's shoulders sagged. "It seemed like a good idea at the time."

"It was a lousy idea. I'm going home." Heather didn't want to, at this hour in the face of a looming snowstorm, but her innate stubbornness refused to yield.

"And waste all that food?" Jason had carried it to the kitchen himself, so he knew exactly what she'd purchased. "I'm cooking, by the way. Which would you prefer, the steak or the salmon?"

Heather's hand flew to her mouth. "I bought enough for four adults for an entire weekend!"

"My point exactly," he said. "We can't leave now. It would be wasteful."

"We can take it home and eat it there. Separately!" Heather climbed to her feet. "We're leaving. If you don't want to get stranded here, I suggest you begin loading the car immediately."

"She's sleeping." He nodded toward Ginger. "I can't believe you'd wake her."

The baby lay curled on the rug, one cheek resting on her arm. A blissful expression transformed her from an active little girl into an angel.

Pride urged Heather to carry through her threat to depart. Common sense disagreed. "I ought to…"

"Have you looked out the window lately?" asked her cheerful tormenter. "It's like one of those fabled Russian white nights you hear about. Surely you're not going to drag us all down the mountainside in a raging blizzard?"

"You planned it this way," she accused, keeping her voice low for the baby's sake.

"That's right, I'm in cahoots with the weather," Jason teased. Did he have to look so relaxed, sitting with his arms circling his knees while the fire crackled?

"If you're expecting a repeat of what happened in Atlanta…"

"Nothing happened in Atlanta," he said. "Isn't that right?"

"It nearly did."

"How nearly?"

"If you still don't remember, I'm not providing any more blow-by-blow descriptions," Heather snapped. "Since you stranded us here, I presume you plan to cook dinner."

"Of course. I volunteered, didn't I?" He sounded less than enthusiastic, though.

Sinking onto the sofa, she indulged in a stretch. "Since, according to you, we're on vacation, I'll be taking a nap. Wake me when the food's ready. I'd prefer salmon to steak tonight."

Something akin to panic fleeted across his darkly handsome face. "No problem. Just tell me how to do it."

"Poach it or bake it or broil it, I don't care." Heather gave an exaggerated yawn, barely remembering in time to cover her mouth. "How about the scalloped potatoes and a salad with it? Sounds good to me." She lowered her lids.

She didn't actually mean to fall asleep, but when she opened her eyes again, Ginger was sitting in the playpen hugging her teddy bear while mouthwatering smells drifted from the kitchen.

Heather checked her watch. She'd been dead to the world for more than half an hour.

For a confused moment, she wondered if Alexei and Lisa had arrived. Then she remembered that not only weren't they coming, they'd never planned on it in the first place.

She almost got angry, except for the evidence that Jason had been working hard while she'd rested. He'd moved Ginger into the safety of the playpen and, judging by the smells, he'd figured out how to cook the meal, too.

Lazily, Heather rose and ambled into the kitchen. His back to her, Jason hummed as he fixed a salad at the counter. On the stove steamed several covered pots.

A laptop computer on the table displayed a recipe for poached salmon. Heather couldn't help being amused at how resourceful Jason had been, going on-line for help rather than waking her.

"Where'd you learn to cook?" she asked.

He tossed a handful of diced cucumber into the salad, then turned to caress her with his gaze. "I hope you slept well."

"Yes, thank you." Belatedly wondering what she must look like, Heather ran a hand through her tousled hair.

"As for the cooking, I picked up a bit here and there," Jason said. "The best I can say for my technique is, I know how to follow a recipe."

"I wondered if your fiancée taught you." Heather dropped the statement like a stone into a pond and waited for the ripples.

"That's a personal subject." His jaw set, Jason lifted a lid from a pot atop the stove. The aroma of poaching salmon and herbs whetted Heather's appetite.

"You're the one who dragged me up here so we could get better acquainted," she reminded him.

Maybe, a small voice warned, she should back off. If they were going to dig into each other's pasts, the truth about Ginger would come out. Well, she'd been thinking about revealing it, anyway, hadn't she? Maybe by tomorrow, if Jason earned her trust, she might be ready to tell him.

Trust had to begin with honesty. He hadn't made a good start of that when he'd tricked her into coming here, but, in her current mood, Heather was willing to give him a second chance.

From a cabinet, Jason extracted a pair of plates and glasses. "You're right. And since the office gossips have probably put me in the worst possible light, I might as well set the record straight."

He arranged two place settings across from each other at the cozy table. Heather found paper napkins in a grocery sack and added cutlery from a drawer.

"Eileen and I drifted into an engagement I wasn't ready for," Jason said. "I know I'm to blame for hurting her, but she wasn't honest about her interests or her goals. It all fell apart during the last year of my residency, when…well, some things went seriously wrong at work that made me take a hard look at myself."

"What kind of things?" Nothing in Jason's professional record hinted at problems, as far as Heather knew.

"One of my patients was a low-income mother-to-be who'd led a rough life." He leaned against the counter. From his remote air, Heather knew he was looking at faces and hearing voices from long ago. "I'd grown up in a privileged environment. Although my parents were too busy to spend much time with me, I'd never even dreamed of the chaos or the abuse she'd grown up with. It rattled me when she talked about it.''

"I understand.'' Heather had been shocked at the circumstances of some of the Moms in Training. Despite the rejections she'd endured during her own unwed pregnancy, her close family had always protected her.

"Although she received free treatment as a charity patient, she couldn't afford vitamins, so I gave her free samples,'' Jason said.

"I did the same thing before I came to Doctors Circle.'' One of the major attractions of working in Serene Beach, for Heather, was that she no longer had to beg and borrow to help underprivileged women. Special funding provided them with medications as well as treatment.

"This girl, Mary Alice, started dropping by to talk, and I sometimes let her hang around my office because she seemed so lonely.'' He removed serving plates from the cabinet.

"It can be hard to know where to draw the line.'' Heather found two bottles of salad dressing and carried them to the table.

"This had been going on for about a month when one of the nurses caught her stealing drugs off a counter. There'd been a few items missing before, including money from purses, but I'd never connected the thefts with Mary Alice.'' Jason transferred the salmon onto a platter. "I felt terrible. I'd exposed the office staff to a thief. To make matters worse, she'd stolen a controlled substance. I could have been in deep water.''

"The only thing you were guilty of was compassion,'' Heather said.

"The hospital administrator read me the riot act.'' Jason's voice grew hoarse, a sign that time hadn't erased the pain he'd experienced years ago. "It made me doubt everything I thought I knew about myself. Although I'd worked hard to succeed, it hadn't been terribly difficult. That was the first time I realized that I could fail. What if they'd yanked my license?"

"That wasn't justified," Heather said.

"Even a temporary suspension would have tarnished my record," Jason said. "If I didn't get the best opportunities, I'd have ended up as just another doctor."

"The world can always use another good doctor." She was glad she'd never felt such an intense drive to be the most distinguished physician in her field. She simply wanted to do her best for her patients.

"That's true, but it isn't enough for me," Jason said. "I was desperate to prove myself, to move on to the next level and never, never make a mistake like that again. When the offer came from the research center in England, I felt as though I'd been given a new lease on life."

"I guess that brings us back to your engagement," Heather said.

"Eileen didn't understand." Jason clicked off the burners under the pots.

"Was she a doctor herself?"

"A law student." He removed the lids and set them aside. "She'd told me she planned to dedicate herself to her career, but that wasn't true. What she'd apparently wanted all along was a husband and kids and a home. I can't blame her, but she picked the wrong guy. I'm afraid I bailed out on her rather abruptly."

"It sounds like neither of you was mature enough to get married," Heather said.

"Looking back, I don't regret breaking it off, but I wish I'd been kinder," Jason said.

"What happened to Mary Alice?"

"She made restitution for the thefts, the drugs were recovered and she was referred to counseling." He placed the hot food on serving dishes. "After that, I lost track of her."

"You want to save every patient, don't you?" Heather said. "I know I do. We're not gods, though. We're just doctors. Well, if we're ready to eat, I'll go get Ginger."

As she went into the living room, she found herself liking Jason more. It was reassuring to discover that he regretted having hurt his fiancée. She also had to admire the compassion he'd showed toward Mary Alice, despite the unpleasant consequences.

Unfortunately, she also saw that sooner or later he would move on to a bigger challenge, a better opportunity. If Boston wasn't big enough for his ambition, Doctors Circle wouldn't be, either. No wonder he had no interest in planting rosebushes.

Regardless of how caring he might be, Jason Carmichael wasn't the kind of man to stick around. That fact bothered Heather more than she wanted it to.

Chapter Eleven

After dinner, Jason moved the playpen to a bedroom and Heather spread a blanket inside it while he held the baby. When she wriggled restlessly, he feared for a moment that he might drop her. Once she nestled into the crook of his arm, however, his uncertainty vanished.

"What's the ritual for putting a baby to bed?" he asked.

Heather gave him a startled glance. "There's not much to it. You change her diaper and lay her down on her back. Why?"

"Surely it involves more than that." Jason refused to accept such an anemic plan for *his* daughter. "In the movie, Mary Poppins sang a lullaby."

"I do that occasionally," Heather admitted. "My voice is nothing to brag about, though."

"You talk with a musical lilt. All you'd have to do is speak the lyrics to her." He'd always enjoyed the texture of her voice.

"Is that a compliment?"

"Well, sure," he said. Concerned that he might be getting too personal for her comfort, Jason added, "Besides, I'm sure babies love the murmur of a woman's voice, regardless of whether she's qualified to sing opera.''

"Men can sing, too." Heather removed most of the toys from the playpen.

"You don't mean me, right?" Jason hadn't performed in public since elementary school, when he'd stumbled through the role of a second molar in a musical play about dental hygiene.

"Do you see any other men around here?"

"Thankfully, no."

"I'm sure Ginger would love to hear you." She folded her arms and fixed him with a commanding stare. "I know I would."

Jason dredged his memory for a song. "Ninety-nine Bottles of Beer on the Wall," which his high-school classmates had bellowed on the bus going to field trips, didn't seem appropriate. "Is it okay if I hum?"

"Sure." Wearing a bemused smile, Heather slid onto the edge of the bed and watched him. Her hair, delightfully mussed, flared around her face like the afterglow of a sunset.

All evening, as they'd talked and eaten and fed the baby, Jason had developed a closeness to her that he'd never experienced before. Not even with Eileen.

He didn't know where it was leading and he didn't care. These moments with his daughter and her mother were so precious, he wished the weekend could last forever.

Rocking Ginger in his arms, he began humming an unidentified tune that popped into his mind. It wasn't much of a melody, more a series of notes that became oddly ominous.

"What on earth is that?" Heather asked.

Jason struggled to identify the song. "It might be the theme from *Jaws*."

"You expect to soothe a baby with that?"

"I didn't realize what it was. Sorry." What kind of father frightened his daughter instead of comforting her? "Okay, I've got a better one."

"You could hardly find a worse one."

He launched into "The Wheels on the Bus," which had stuck in his mind after listening to a patient, a year or so ago, repeat it endlessly to keep her toddler quiet.

The effect on Ginger was electrifying. About to doze off, she snapped to attention. That might be because Jason instinctively circled her through the air to illustrate how the wheels went round and round.

"Wait!" Heather said. "I was wrong."

"About what?"

"You did find a worse one." Reaching out, she pried the baby from his grasp. "The object is to lull the little one to sleep, not rev her up to party all night."

"You mean I fail Lullaby?" Jason asked.

"It's okay. Nobody expects the irascible Dr. Carmichael to turn into Daddy Dearest, although I do appreciate the effort." Gazing deep into the baby's green eyes, Heather launched into the old song, "Mockingbird."

Ginger's muscles relaxed and within minutes she sank into a doze. Cradling her, Heather glowed with love.

Jason had never seen a woman look more beautiful. Ladies in formfitting evening gowns or skimpy swimsuits didn't compare to Heather in an untucked blouse and creased slacks. Motherhood transformed her into a force both universal and very, very specific.

He remembered the first time he'd seen her, in Atlanta. He'd noticed instantly that she had a special quality. It had amazed him that every man in the hotel lobby didn't try to corral her for himself.

After that, images blurred. Drinks and conversation. The elevator to his room. A glimpse of a butterfly. Then, frustratingly, nothing. His body throbbed with a longing to replace that nothingness with tangible memories.

As the baby drooped into sleep, Heather lowered her gently to the blanket. Ginger nestled into the softness.

Finger to lips, Heather led the way out. In the living room, the fire crackled, its warmth a delicious contrast to the wind rattling the windows.

"This weather seems so exotic to me." Through the glass, Heather regarded the snow swirling in the darkness. "For a Bostonian like you, I guess it's normal."

"I haven't been snowed in for quite a while." Jason almost hoped the forecast was wrong and the storm would continue tomorrow as well. Then there'd be no chance of leaving. "Hold on a minute."

In the kitchen, he found a bottle of wine he'd spied earlier and returned carrying it and a couple of glasses. "This is what was missing."

"I'm not sure that's such a good idea." Heather regarded him with a mixture of amusement and doubt. "Neither of us handles alcohol well, judging by the way we behaved in Atlanta."

"What's the worst that could happen?" Jason asked.

"Do I have to spell it out?" Heather said.

"No. My memory of what happened may be fuzzy, but I get the idea." Setting the bottle aside, he made himself comfortable on the couch. "I don't know why, but being around you puts my best intentions in jeopardy."

"Are you saying it's my fault if anything happens?" Heather eyed the bottle and the empty glasses beside it.

"Not at all." Jason raised one hand for a truce. He didn't understand why everything he said came out wrong around this woman. "That's not what I meant. I'm a grown man. I take responsibility for my own actions."

"Then do you promise to behave if I have a few drops?" Cautiously, she reached for a glass.

"I'll do my best." Jason fully intended to hold himself in check.

"Okay. It *is* Friday night, after all." After pouring herself some wine, Heather slipped into a chair and curled her slim legs beneath her. She'd discarded her shoes, he noticed.

Her feet were long and slender. Perfect for running on the beach or tangling in the sheets. The amazing part was that they sparkled.

"Are those stars on your toenails?" Jason asked in surprise.

"I had them done on impulse," Heather said. "My dau—" She stopped, and quickly found new words. "They're a silly indulgence, but Ginger finds them fascinating."

Although he pretended not to notice the slip, Jason's heart leaped. Once again, Heather had confirmed that she had a daughter.

He followed her example and poured himself some wine. Not being a connoisseur, he didn't know much about bouquet, but it tasted good to him. "You made an excellent choice."

"The only other option was flowers."

Her answer made no sense. "Flowers instead of wine?"

"No, instead of stars." Heather blinked. "You were talking about the wine? Okay, I'm making the shift from pedicures now. It's from one of my favorite California vintners.''

"Is that where you're from? The wine country?" Jason asked.

Heather laughed. "Northridge is nowhere near the Napa or Sonoma valleys. My parents drove us up there on vacation when I was a teenager, but I was too young to visit the wine-tasting rooms.''

"That's too bad," he said. "Maybe you should pay the wineries another visit. I'd like to visit the Bay Area while I'm in California.''

They talked about favorite places to visit. Jason's ranged from Washington, D.C., and Colonial Williamsburg to London and Stonehenge. Heather's lay closer to home: Catalina Island, Santa Barbara, Mexico.

Slowly, the tension between them dissolved into easy comradeship. Jason's subtle awareness of Heather's femininity remained a pleasant undertone.

In the bedroom, Ginger slept soundly. Heather checked on her the first time and Jason the second. The third time, they went in together.

It would be a natural time to bring up the subject closest to his heart. Not that he'd plied Heather with wine in hopes of encouraging her to admit he was Ginger's father, but it might work out that way.

He didn't say anything, though. There was too great a risk of spoiling the mood. Perhaps by tomorrow she'd raise the subject herself.

As they were finishing their second glasses, Heather abruptly sat upright. "I don't believe it!''

"What?" Jason glanced around, trying to figure out what had stirred her response.

"The snow stopped.''

Through the window, he saw that she was right. "The

roads can't be cleared yet. Please don't tell me you're thinking of driving down the mountain tonight.''

"Not in a million years." Heather stretched languorously, a movement that displayed her shapely body to advantage. "I've got the funniest idea."

"What's that?" Rising heat inside Jason tempted him to make a suggestion of his own. He squelched the idea.

"I always wanted to make a snow angel but I never got the chance," she said. "Do you think we could?"

"Now?" It was after ten o'clock. On the other hand, a bit of a chill might dampen his ardor.

"You're right. The whole notion is goofy." Heather gave a little shake that made her hair bounce. "I should wait for tomorrow."

"Maybe there is no tomorrow."

"Excuse me?"

"That's the wine speaking," Jason admitted. "On the other hand, if there's something you've always wanted to do and the opportunity presents itself, why wait?"

"It's not as if a warm spell is going to set in while we sleep," Heather pointed out, evidently still battling her impulse.

"It's something you've always wanted to do," he persisted.

"I was being childish," she said. "It's much too late at night to go running around in the snow."

Jason told himself she was right. They were two distinguished physicians, for heaven's sake. They ought to behave themselves with decorum. Or forget all about decorum and rip each other's clothes off.

No, no, no. He was *not* going to think along those lines.

Snow angels. He hadn't made one since he was—how old? Twelve, maybe. That was when his father had de-

clared that it was beneath his son's dignity to roll around
in the snow like a little kid.

Longing welled for the days of childhood that had
ended in seventh grade as, one by one, his parents declared him too old. Too old for his teddy bears. Too old
to read his favorite children's books. Too old for snow
angels.

Jason pushed off from the arm of the sofa, arriving at
an upright state despite the liquidity of his knees. "I'm
going to do it," he declared.

"Do what?"

"I haven't been allowed to make a snow angel since
I was in junior high school," Jason said. "The time has
come for a relapse."

"Your parents wouldn't let you play in the snow? I
understand their reasoning for not allowing a dog, but
surely they weren't afraid you'd track snow through their
picture-perfect house," Heather said.

"My father said I'd become a young man and it was
time I learned to control myself," Jason recalled. "He
made it sound as if I might disgrace the family."

"By frolicking?" Heather asked in disbelief.

"My father frowned upon frolicking. He frowned
upon almost any form of fun." Jason knew he was exaggerating. His father was neither a Puritan nor a tyrant.
But he *had* been overly strict.

"You need to get in touch with your inner child."
Heather grimaced. "I can't believe I said that. What a
cliché!"

Jason's inner child, or whatever had risen from his
subconscious, urged him not to let this moment pass.
"My coat," he said, and headed for the entryway.

"Wait for me!" Heather jumped up.

Jason zipped his jacket and pushed open the front

door. Cold air stung his face and filled his lungs while, in the fragments of sky visible through the cloud cover, he glimpsed an infinity of stars.

A bemittened figure in a parka darted beneath his upraised arm and out onto the smooth white expanse. When Heather turned, starlight glinted on her teeth. "It's perfect! How do I do this?"

She reminded him of a creature from a fairy tale as she twirled against the whiteness, radiating joy. There was something magical about this woman.

"If you don't quit dancing around, you'll destroy your work surface," Jason instructed, although he doubted there was any sight on earth the angels would enjoy more than that of Heather cavorting in the moonlight.

"Sorry." She halted.

"Stand in a clear patch, sit down carefully and lie on your back," he instructed. "Wave your arms straight up and down and shift your legs."

Heather obeyed. Despite a tug of embarrassment, Jason followed suit.

The snow tickled his neck with a cold kiss. He felt awkward at first, scissoring his arms and legs, but Heather's whoops of pleasure encouraged him. Tension vanished and he recovered the loose-limbed freedom of a child.

After making the angel, he lay flat on his back staring at the heavens. The clouds parted bit by bit, revealing more brilliant lights beyond. Jason made out the Big Dipper and Andromeda.

"It's as if God is pulling back the curtains," Heather said.

"You can see the constellations with remarkable clarity." Jason's father had spent many a summer night instructing him on how to chart the heavens through his telescope.

"Forget the constellations," Heather said. "This is not a scientific expedition. Enjoy the beauty."

Jason blinked. In place of constellations, he saw a wild swirling realm filled with mystery and the possibility of distant worlds.

When he was little, he'd longed to fly through space and time, to soar in the night and step into enchanted lands. At his parents' insistence, he'd put all that fantasizing behind him.

Tonight, Heather's enthusiasm restored his sense of wonder. An obscuring layer inside him separated like the clouds, allowing Jason to touch his own imagination.

In vino, veritas. The Latin phrase made sense to him as it never had before, that truth could be found with the aid of wine. And, he added silently, with the help of a special woman.

"You're right," he said. "It's absolutely gorgeous out here."

"It really is," Heather said. A long moment passed while they studied the twinkling stars. Peace drifted into Jason's heart. He never wanted to move again.

"I hate to admit it," said his companion, "but I'm getting cold."

"Of course you're cold. You're lying in the snow," Jason pointed out. At the same time, he became aware that his gloved hands were growing numb and his nose smarted.

"I can't get up," Heather said.

"I'll help." He started to rise.

"No!" She waved a hand frantically. "I meant, I can't get up without ruining the angel."

"We can make more tomorrow," Jason said.

"If we wreck them, what's the point?" Heather asked gloomily. "We came out here for nothing."

"The point is to exist in the moment," he told her. "Once it's over, we have to go on to the next thing and not look back."

It was a philosophy he'd heard about but never been able to implement in his own life. Tonight, beneath the benevolent influence of the stars, he decided to turn over a new leaf.

He regretted hurting Eileen and he rued his mistake with Mary Alice. But it was time to let go of his guilt and move on.

At that moment, a burden seemed to lift from his shoulders. Ten years was long enough to berate himself for errors in judgment. Jason felt light enough to float.

"I like that idea." Heather gave a contented sigh. "Think of how much anxiety we'd spare ourselves if we didn't worry over the past."

"Or the future. Except the immediate future, when we're likely to freeze to death if we don't move." Rousing himself, he jumped to his feet. Heather followed suit. "Remember: Don't look back and don't look down."

"I never got to see my angel," she said wistfully.

"You *were* the angel," he said. "Isn't that better?"

"I'm looking down, whether you like it or not." She turned. "Oh, it's splendid!"

Following her gaze, he saw that they hadn't ruined the angels after all. "They're lovely."

"Yours is better than mine." She pointed to it. "You have crisper edges."

"I make a good angel." He grinned.

"No one at work would believe it." Heather shot him an impish grin. "Does this mean you're going to be sweetness and light from now on?"

"Only when I'm intoxicated with wine and a celestial influence."

"We'd better go in." Heather sounded reluctant, although she was hugging herself against the chill. "We might not hear Ginger if she wakes up. Besides, my feet are turning into blocks of ice." She started forward, then staggered.

Jason seized her elbow just as Heather's leg buckled. If he hadn't caught her, he was almost certain she would have fallen.

Also, if he hadn't caught her, his nose wouldn't have buried itself in the frizzy hair bursting around the fringes of her parka. His arms wouldn't have scooped her close and electricity wouldn't have sizzled through him as their bodies came together.

He felt her pulse pounding and her breathing quicken. The heat of their responses seared away the chill.

"I don't know what happened," Heather said breathlessly. "My feet must have fallen asleep."

"Put your hands around my neck." Hesitantly, she obeyed. Jason slid an arm beneath her and gathered her against his chest. "Hang on."

"You're not really going to carry me!"

"It sure looks that way, doesn't it?" he replied, cherishing the weight and the softness of her.

"You'll never make it." Heather clung to him, either from tenderness or fear. He hoped it was the former.

"Fortunately, you're half my size." In Jason's current heated state, he had no trouble blazing a path across the snow and into the house. If he'd checked back, he was sure he'd see a path of melted slush.

In the entryway, he lowered Heather to the floor but maintained a tight grip. For support, he told himself.

As a doctor, he knew he ought to wrap her in blankets

and bring her a hot drink to restore her temperature. There was a better way to warm up, however. Quicker, too.

"What are you doing?" Heather whispered as he unzipped her parka and slipped his hands inside.

"Frostbite therapy." Jason's mouth found hers, steaming away the coolness and arousing the heat within.

For a heartbeat, Heather resisted. Then her hand found the back of his neck and stroked the sensitive strip below the hairline. Her fingers followed it to the edge of his jaw as her tongue met his in a moment of surrender.

The only question was, which one of them was surrendering? Jason wondered, and realized he no longer cared.

IN THAT INSTANT, Heather remembered everything about Jason. The soft tickle of his hair. The probing allure of his kiss. The heady blend of aftershave lotion and male fervor.

Even though she'd been tempted many times these past few weeks to give the man a slap, an undercurrent of desire had underscored every encounter. She'd fought it, trying to deny his powerful appeal. Yet everything about him drew her: his confidence, his brilliance, his magnetic green eyes.

Tonight, in addition, she'd discovered a new side of Jason. He sang to babies, even if he did have odd taste in music. He'd proved resourceful in the kitchen and playful in the snow. And he fit into her embrace as if he'd been born for it.

They stumbled up the stairs together, pausing at the halfway point for another kiss. Ruefully, Heather reflected that she was probably going to regret this. Oh, well. If she never did anything she regretted, wouldn't life be boring?

Standing two steps above Jason brought her face-to-face with him. "I like being your height for a change," she teased.

"I like it, too." He unfastened the buttons on her blouse and blew softly, maddeningly into the cleavage above her bra. When he smoothed down the straps and tasted her nipples, heat raged through her like wildfire.

Heather ran her hands across Jason's muscular shoulders and down to his waist, relishing the answering shudders that ran through him. Boldly, she slid off her blouse and her bra, and reached for him again.

He trailed kisses down her throat. When his hands claimed her breasts, she sank onto the stairs and had to grab a baluster to keep from sliding down.

"Maybe we should..." The words died in Heather's throat as her slacks and panties disappeared into the void below. "I mean, the bed might be more..."

"Who needs a bed?" growled Jason.

Laughter bubbled inside her. If she'd known how much fun he could be, her disappointment on finding him asleep in Atlanta would have been even keener.

A moment later, his own clothes followed hers over the railing. Despite the discomfort of the stairs beneath her, Heather enjoyed a sense of daring.

Jason moved like a tiger, his body rubbing hers sensuously. Heather felt the teeth beneath his lips and the urgency of his hands gripping her bottom as he lifted her to him. The riser digging into her back provided only a faint counterpoint to the reactions rioting through the rest of her.

"We should..." *Take precautions.*

"...never stop," he finished. Poising overhead, he

filled her easily, completely, with himself. A gasp spun from Heather. When he pulled out, she missed him.

"Do that again."

"My pleasure." Holding her hips, he entered her once more. This time the sensation was gentler, yet, if anything, more intense. Heather moaned.

Brushing a kiss across her nose, Jason moved in and out. He threw his head back and, with lids lowered, lost himself in sheer bliss. The pleasure of watching him was almost as great for Heather as her own overwhelming hunger.

Forget caution. Forget how wise they were both supposed to be. Arching her back, she matched his movements with her own until the world disappeared and they entered into a steamy, private heaven.

Chapter Twelve

Fulfillment. Jason hadn't truly known what it meant until this moment.

He hovered on the brink of it, fighting the compulsion to plunge over the edge. His entire being crackled with a single impulse, a single need. Yet every sense remained attuned to Heather. His sensitivity to her might have been alarming if it didn't feel so absolutely right.

He was still trying to hold back when her fingers gripped his buttocks and she wriggled against him. A wall of pleasure sent him barreling off a cliff in freefall. Heather's cries nearly drowned beneath his hoarse groans as they clung to each other, all the way to a deliriously soft landing.

They lay sprawled on the staircase, pulses thundering. The first word that scraped its way clear of Jason's throat was "Unbelievable."

He sensed rather than saw Heather's smile. "We're lucky Alexei and Lisa didn't decide to drop by after all. This would be hard to explain." Jason gathered her against him and wondered if there had ever been a funnier, sweeter, sexier woman in the history of the world.

THEY MADE IT to the bedroom at last. Lying with her head on Jason's chest, Heather listened to the evenness of his breathing and waited for sleep to claim her.

They'd shared something tonight that ran deeper than a casual encounter. He'd felt it, too, she was certain.

She tried not to think about what might happen as a result. Perhaps, this time, there wouldn't be any emotional fallout. Surely she hadn't misjudged Jason's capacity for intimacy.

A momentary uneasiness disturbed her tranquility. They'd forgotten to take precautions. What if something came of it?

Unlikely, she told herself. As an infertility doctor, she knew the odds were against her conceiving from a single act of lovemaking. But it also only took one time.

A longing jolted through her, keen as a scalpel. A baby. Would she ever have one to keep? To nurture a child through the miraculous stages of growth would be a joy almost as great as finding the love of her life. Was it possible she might have both?

Heather snuggled closer to Jason. She yearned to hear him say he loved her. She ached to see the same light in his face tomorrow morning that had been there tonight, to know that he treasured her beyond reason.

Keeping that hope in mind, she relaxed and fell asleep.

JASON AWOKE to an early-morning glow filtering through the skylight. Despite a few twinges in his temples from the wine he'd drunk last night, he was bursting with energy.

During the night, Heather had rolled away from him. He smiled at the sight of her slender back and a couple of freckles visible on one shoulder. She was his snow angel and his sun sprite at the same time.

Remembering that they weren't alone, he got up without disturbing her and went quietly downstairs. Outside, sun shimmered across the snow, turning its surface to diamonds. In the baby's room, Ginger lay sleeping, a tiny copy of her mother.

Moisture blurred Jason's gaze. What more could a man ask than this peaceful oneness with his family? And why had it taken him so long to realize it?

Upstairs again, he found Heather blinking herself awake. "Ginger's still in slumberland." Slipping into bed, he pulled the sheets and quilt over his legs.

"Thanks for checking." She watched him uncertainly.

He mulled over whether to kiss any trace of unhappiness from her face, and reluctantly concluded that honest discussion was a wiser course. "Is something worrying you?"

"I was afraid you might snap at me," she said. "Like last time."

"I was an idiot last time." That was putting it mildly, he thought. The man he'd been in Atlanta a mere fifteen months ago seemed like a complete stranger. "I can't believe my brain blocked out the memory of making love to you. Last night was incredible, yet I'd have sworn it was our first time."

"It *was* our first time." A familiar pucker formed between Heather's eyebrows. "I thought we'd gotten that straight."

He couldn't go on pretending. "I think it's time we laid our cards on the table."

"What card game did you have in mind?" As she spoke, she sat up, revealing a luscious pair of pink-tipped breasts.

"Strip poker?" Jason teased, thoroughly distracted from his train of thought.

Her expression lightened. "I'd say stud poker was more like it."

"Suits me." He ruffled her springy hair and moved closer. Forget the chitchat. Nothing brought two people closer than making love.

As his hand slid toward those luscious orbs, Heather gripped his wrist. "You were right. We need to talk first."

"I'd rather…"

"I know what you'd rather do. So would I. But we need to clear the air about this false idea you've got."

"We'll have plenty of time to talk later." Jason remembered his new philosophy of living in the moment. In the morning light, he approved of it even more than he had last evening.

"My mind is racing," Heather said. "I've got to say what I have to say, or I'll keep interrupting you."

"If you insist." Reluctantly, he sat back.

"You need to accept the truth," she said. "You fell asleep and, the next morning, you gave me the cold shoulder. End of story."

Briefly, Jason considered pretending to agree so they could proceed to something far more important: making love. But that wasn't why they'd come here this weekend, he reminded himself. It was time to get to the point, although he preferred to ease into the subject diplomatically.

"I'm afraid that wasn't the end of the story. You know it, and now I know it, too," he said. "It was Quentin Ladd who gave me the final clue."

"You've lost me." Heather rested her cheek on her knees as she listened. "The clue to what?"

"Last weekend, Quent and I went out for breakfast." Jason wanted to tell the whole story of how he'd figured out about Ginger, step by step, so she'd understand that he hadn't been snooping or indulging in idle gossip.

"I'm glad to hear you shared in some male bonding, but Quent doesn't know anything about Atlanta," Heather said. "Nobody does."

He wasn't sure what to make of that remark so he let it go. The point was to reach the next level, the one on which she acknowledged him as Ginger's father. "He told me about how clueless Patrick was when Natalie got pregnant."

"Yes, that story has already passed into Doctors Circle lore," she said drily. "So?"

"Edith told me how you took two months leave last fall for personal reasons," he said. Heather simply sat watching him. Surely by now she caught his drift! "I may be as clueless as Patrick in some respects, but I can add."

"I'm afraid I'm slow on the uptake today." Heather tilted her head quizzically. "You'll have to spell this out."

"Eight months after we supposedly didn't make love in Atlanta, you went on leave," Jason said.

"And?"

"And you came back with a baby who has your red hair and my green eyes," he said.

Heather's jaw dropped. Jason hoped she wasn't going to continue denying the truth.

"What conclusion did you draw?" she said.

"You know what conclusion I drew!"

"Humor me," she said.

"If you insist." Determined not to provoke a fight, he said slowly and patiently, "Ginger is my daughter. And yours, of course."

She watched him with an unreadable expression.

"Tell me something," she said. "Where does Olive fit into this scenario?"

"I figure she's the nanny." He supposed he might have guessed wrong there. "Or she might be your niece, as you said. But she doesn't resemble Ginger in the least, and she takes off whenever she feels like it. I mean, honestly, you can't expect me to believe that you're this devoted to your great-niece."

A half-dozen emotions flitted across Heather's face, from amusement to dismay. "You've concluded that I not only had your baby but also kept my pregnancy secret from the entire staff at Doctors Circle except maybe Quentin Ladd?"

"That about sums it up." Jason wished he weren't getting an uneasy feeling from her reaction. Still, he didn't see what other conclusion he could have drawn.

The warmth drained from Heather's expression. "Wait a minute. Is that why you brought me here this weekend, to soften me up so I'd confirm that Ginger is your daughter?"

Although Jason was sorry if he'd made her angry, he wished she'd quit toying with him and come clean. "I didn't plan what happened between us. I simply hoped that once you felt comfortable with me, you'd open up."

"You weren't falling in love with me last night," she said, more to herself than to him. "You were winning over the mother of your child. I'll give you credit. You've apparently taken a shine to Ginger."

"Of course I have." This conversation wasn't tracking the way Jason had hoped. Although he hated to spoil any remaining trace of the tenderness between them, he decided to press the point until Heather quit denying the obvious. "Under the circumstances, I forgive you for keeping me in the dark, but I'm entitled to share my daughter's life. She's part of me, part of my genetic background, part of my future.''

"What about me?" Despite the evenness of tone, her voice struck him as dangerously low. "Where do I fit into this charming picture?"

"You're her mother, of course." Jason didn't understand her anger. What had he done wrong? "I want the whole package. I want my family." It was as close to a declaration of love as he knew how to make.

Whatever he'd expected, it hadn't been this look of sheer disgust. "You mean, you want us as long as we don't get in the way of your ambitions, right?"

"My ambitions are irrelevant," he said, bewildered.

"Not to *your family*." She gave the words a puzzling emphasis. "You don't want to buy a house or plant flowers because it might tie you down. You have to be free to pursue professional opportunities anywhere in the world so you won't end up being merely a good doctor. Did I get any of that wrong?"

Jason scratched his ear as he tried to figure out what had ticked her off. "I confess, I haven't thought the whole thing through."

"You don't really want a family," Heather said. "Or a woman who's anything more than a temporary convenience. What this whole weekend has been about is securing your title to your genetic heritage."

"Wait a minute!" How on earth had she gotten so far off course? "That's not true."

"I can't believe I let you fool me this way." She bristled with outrage. "First you lure me up here on a pretext and then it turns out you had a hidden motive the whole time. 'Establish a professional relationship,' my foot! You didn't even want to establish a personal relationship. All you want is to stake a claim to your DNA.''

Jason raised his hands to stop the onslaught of words. ''Let's be rational about this. I don't want to have to take you to court, Heather.''

''Take me to court?'' She gave a bitter laugh. ''Just a minute.'' Throwing off the covers, she hopped up, not seeming to care that she was stark naked. ''Don't go anywhere.''

''I wasn't planning on it.''

She vanished down the stairs. Jason punched a pillow into position against the headboard and tried to figure out how this conversation had veered 180 degrees from common sense.

He didn't view his daughter as a vessel for his DNA. He wanted to be her daddy, to read stories to her and, when she got older, to give her boyfriends the third degree, like a father on an old-fashioned TV sitcom.

As for Heather, the last thing he'd had in mind was treating her as a convenience. She was the most inconvenient woman he'd ever met. Of course, he conceded, that wasn't what mattered.

True, he hadn't given any thought to what a relationship with her might entail. A man didn't have to plan out every moment of his life in advance, did he?

Heather reappeared. Although he'd half expected to see her carrying her daughter, there was no sign of the baby. ''Is she still sleeping?''

''She's playing happily. I gave her a few more toys.'' Heather plopped onto the quilt and handed him a photograph. ''Look at this.''

It was a wedding picture, the kind shot with an instant camera. The bride, whom he recognized as Olive, beamed at the lens. The groom smiled down at the baby in his arms. The child was instantly recognizable as Ginger.

"Okay, so it was Olive's wedding you went to in Las Vegas," Jason said. "I still don't get it. Why is her husband holding Ginger?"

"Notice anything about his coloring?" Heather demanded.

"He's got red hair." You couldn't miss that.

"I'm sorry his eye color doesn't show up. It's a splendid shade of green," she said.

"So who is he? Besides being Olive's groom?" Jason wished the guy would disappear, that the entire photo would vanish, that this conversation had never taken place. Or, rather, that it was going in the direction he was absolutely convinced it should be taking.

"He's Ginger's father," Heather said.

"I'm Ginger's father!"

"His name is John Hiram," Heather said. "He just mustered out of the marines and married Olive. She has his coloring. Not mine and not yours."

This man couldn't be Ginger's father. Jason's brain immediately hit upon a flaw in Heather's account. "If they're Ginger's parents, why is she staying with you this weekend?"

"Because they're on their honeymoon," she said.

Oh, right. He'd forgotten about honeymoons.

Yet none of this made sense. The reality he'd accepted last Sunday had become so much a part of Jason's world view that even this evidence in his hand couldn't instantly dispel it.

He had a daughter. He'd fallen in love with her, and looked forward to years of playtime and cuddling. How could all that vanish because of a photograph?

Jason struggled to consider the possibility that the

puzzle pieces that had slid so neatly together also fit a completely different picture. Although, as a scientist, he relied upon his powers of deductive reasoning, it was beginning to seem as if he'd gone agonizingly astray.

However, Heather still hadn't tied up all the loose threads. Perhaps this was simply a dodge to throw him off the scent.

"You're telling me that the timing was pure coincidence." Jason didn't try to repress the irony in his tone. "It just so happened that eight or nine months after we met, your niece gave birth. As her aunt, you decided to leave your patients for two months to be with her and then, afterward, invited her to live with you. I have to say, that's pretty darn generous of you. There can't be very many aunts like you in the world."

Heather flushed crimson. No one but a redhead could turn that color, Jason reflected. If they hadn't both been in such dismal moods, he'd have told her she looked like a rose.

"There is one point of the story that I haven't been honest about," she said.

"Aha!"

"Don't 'aha!' me!" Heather retorted.

"Can't a man say 'aha!' when an important revelation is about to be made?"

"No, because you're being sarcastic," she said. "Now listen carefully. Only a very few people at Doctors Circle know what I'm about to tell you, and if you don't mind your manners, you won't be one of them."

Jason decided to obey, even though he found her logic hard to follow. "Shoot." He leaned against the pillow, holding on to a tendril of hope.

Perhaps, miraculously, this latest revelation would change everything back to the way it had been earlier this morning. He wanted his adorable daughter back. He wanted his warm relationship with her beautiful mother, too.

"The short version is, I got pregnant when I was a teenager and relinquished the baby for adoption," Heather said. "That baby was Olive."

"She has dark hair." He wanted this story not to be true. Oh, how badly he wanted that.

"Her father, who was a father in name only, had dark hair," she said. "Last year, Olive contacted me. Her adoptive parents had died and John was overseas, so I went to be with her during the birth. I invited her to stay with me while she finished college."

"Olive's your daughter." If he repeated the words often enough, maybe they'd finally sink in.

"I don't know if my redheaded genes skipped a generation or if she got her hair from John," Heather said. "Ginger did inherit his eyes, since mine and Olive's are brown. End of story."

Despite his reluctance to believe it, the story made sense. It tied up the loose threads, leaving no strand that even a desperate father could cling to.

A desperate non-father, apparently. Jason couldn't fully absorb his loss in a single moment.

He bowed his head in a gesture of defeat. "I guess I've been acting like an idiot. That seems to be a habit with me where you're concerned."

"That would be an understatement." Heather didn't intend to go easy on him, obviously.

Jason wanted the other Heather back, the woman who'd thrown herself into his arms last night. He missed her playfulness and their emotional closeness.

He also missed the bond that had begun to form between him and Ginger. "Is there any chance you'll be raising the baby yourself?"

"I'm afraid not. She's moving to Texas with her parents after they return on Monday," Heather said. "I don't even get to watch my granddaughter grow up."

"Your granddaughter," Jason repeated. His brain chugged along, barely functioning.

"I suppose it's time I let the gossips at Doctors Circle know about my past." Heather stood up, taking the photograph with her. "Maybe I should hold a press conference. Better idea: I'll let Cynthia spread the word. She's normally discreet but she can put a bug in a few indiscreet ears."

"People at Doctors Circle have indiscreet ears?" It was easier to joke about absurdities than to accept the fact that he had no claim on Ginger. Or on Heather, either.

"Are you planning to make fun of everything I say?" she snapped.

"I wasn't making fun. I'm a little confused," Jason admitted.

"Sorry to disappoint you, but you'll get over it," she said. "Now I suggest we go downstairs and fix breakfast before we head home. It's a good thing we didn't bother to unpack, isn't it?"

"I suppose so." He couldn't summon the willpower to move. After a moment, she whisked away.

Jason listened to the rustle of her bare feet going down to the first floor and heard the baby's happy babble rise in greeting. He pictured Heather lifting the little girl from her playpen and giving her a hug.

No wonder she loved the child so much. That was how grandmothers were supposed to act.

He felt bereft. It was ridiculous, Jason supposed. He

hadn't actually lost anything, yet his heart told him otherwise.

For a little while, he'd been both a daddy and a lover. He'd had a family and a future filled with special moments. He missed his illusion.

He'd lost something else, too. This weekend, Heather had given him another chance, which he'd ruined by laying his assumptions on her. Where did they go from here? That was up to her, and he got the distinct impression she wanted nothing further to do with him.

He'd let his emotions get the better of his judgment. As with Eileen and Mary Alice, it had been a mistake.

With a wrench, Jason tried to release the dream he'd nurtured so intensely. This wasn't going to be easy. Still, he couldn't afford the luxury of wallowing in his disappointment.

In the next few months, he faced a tremendous challenge. With the clinic opening, he'd have to juggle administrative tasks, the needs of his staff and the demands of his medical practice. Jason had to be prepared to devote as many hours as necessary, including evenings and weekends, to his job.

He thought of Eva LoBianco, brimming with the hope of having another child, and of Loretta, agonizingly afraid she might never be a mother. As he recalled his delight in Ginger, the child who had almost been his, his heart twisted with longing.

It occurred to him that, for the first time, he had an inkling of how his patients actually felt.

As SHE DROVE down the mountain, Heather held herself rigidly in check. She refrained from glancing at Jason, who'd chosen to sit beside her this time instead of in the back.

However, he'd helped feed the baby at breakfast and had carried her to the car. Heather could almost have sworn he'd studied the little girl wistfully. Under other circumstances, she might have spared him some sympathy.

What stopped her was the knowledge that he'd never given Heather a moment's consideration in all his machinations. He'd lured her to the cabin on false pretenses and made love to her under the guise of wanting her for herself, when what he'd really wanted was to take possession of Ginger.

"I'm sorry," Jason said into the silence.

"You should be." Heather's chest squeezed every time she remembered her foolish hope that he might love her.

"I don't just mean I'm sorry that Ginger isn't my daughter." His rich voice contained a thoughtful note. "I'm sorry for the distress I've caused you."

"I'll survive." She wished she weren't so aware of his arm flung across the seat back, inches from her neck. It made the hairs prickle. And it made her want to rub her cheek against his skin and invite him back into her bed.

"If you like, I'll make a full confession to Patrick," he said. "Although all I told him was that I planned to use it to boost morale."

"You certainly didn't boost my morale."

"You have every right to be furious with me." Jason sounded so crestfallen that she decided to give him a break. Besides, she had no desire for the details of their encounter to become known around Doctors Circle.

"As for what happened between us, it's none of his business," Heather said. "As far as I'm concerned, we went to the mountains to talk about the clinic, and that's what we did.''

''You have grounds to file a personnel complaint against me,'' Jason said. ''I wouldn't blame you.''

''Quit trying to act humble. It doesn't suit you.'' She checked on Ginger in the rearview mirror. The little girl was gazing peacefully out the window. ''It's kind of funny, when you come to think about it.''

''It is?''

''You put the clues together in a logical sequence.'' On reviewing his statements while she was showering, Heather had been amused to see how neatly the facts fit into his erroneous conclusion. ''I suppose from your perspective you were trying to do the right thing.''

''At this point, I'm not going to defend myself,'' Jason said glumly. ''I should have approached you in a dignified manner and voiced my concerns. From now on, I assure you, I'll behave the way a fellow professional ought to.''

Unexpectedly, disappointment twisted in Heather's stomach. Annoying as she sometimes found his habit of popping up in her private life, she enjoyed it, too. Scenes flashed across her mental screen: Jason smuggling the puppy under his jacket, Jason cycling beside her at the health spa, Jason helping her make angels in the snow.

Above all, Jason making love to her.

She was going to miss his affection. Well, so what? Heather asked herself sternly. This man would depart for another corner of the world whenever it suited his career.

It was only a question of when he would break her heart, not if. She chose to get it over with now. So what if she lost the possibility of a few more delirious weekends and nights together? Giving him up without delay was for the best, in the long run.

She kept reminding herself of that all the way to Serene Beach.

Chapter Thirteen

Jason stood in the hallway, reading Loretta's chart while medical personnel bustled around him. In the three weeks since his weekend with Heather, the clinic had been transformed from bare-bones to fully operational.

It was now officially open, although without fanfare until next month's conclusion of the Endowment Fund drive. Since he was so busy he barely slept, Jason didn't mind the delay.

He did mind the distance that had formed between him and Heather. His world still hadn't shifted back to normal. He found himself looking for the source of every childish cry he overheard, and aching with memories whenever Heather breezed past him in the corridor.

Still, he'd behaved himself, as promised. He didn't drop into her new corner office without good reason, and he kept their conversations factual.

All the while, he missed the flash of her smile and the soft luxury of her body pressing against his. He missed the spontaneity of flinging themselves into the snow. He missed the scent of her hair.

Thank goodness there was little time to dwell on what he'd lost. Alexei and Lisa had arrived and taken on patients from the long lists of applicants. Jason's own early patients had undergone their initial two-week cycles of hormonal treatments, and Eric Wong and his associates were busily growing embryos.

Not just embryos—children, many of whom would develop into boys and girls, active, lovable and inquisitive like the babies on the mural. Like Ginger.

Gathering his thoughts, Jason flipped the chart shut and went into the examining room. Loretta, the white streak standing out vividly in her dark hair, sat with hands clasped. As before, she'd chosen to come by herself.

"How are my embryos?" Awaiting his answer, she pressed her lips together so tightly they turned white.

Jason wished he had better news. "I believe we've found the cause of your infertility," he said gently.

"Is it fixable?"

"Possibly." He sat on a stool facing her, aware that she deserved the unvarnished truth yet sorry that, at the very least, there wasn't going to be a pregnancy this cycle.

"Go on," the public relations director said.

"Your embryos aren't developing well." That was devastating news, and Jason hurried to explain. "Often when that happens, it's because of some genetic problem that can't be fixed. However, there's nothing wrong with your embryos genetically."

"Then why aren't they developing?" Despite Loretta's poise, a quaver betrayed her anxiety.

"In cases like this, the cause is sometimes found in the cytoplasm. That's the fluid around the nucleus of the egg. It contains mitochondria, which provide energy. Basically, the cytoplasm supports the development of the nucleus."

"Skip the science lesson," Loretta said. "What's the bottom line?"

"The next step would be to transfer cytoplasm into your eggs from a donor egg," Jason said. "The result would be a child with your and your husband's genetic heritage, along with a small trace of the donor's DNA."

"This sounds like science fiction," Loretta said.

"Not long ago, it was."

She frowned. "Does it work?"

"There have been successful pregnancies," Jason said.

"How many?"

He didn't want to sugarcoat the facts. "I can't give you odds on this one. We know the technique works, but it isn't perfected."

"I'm tired of being a guinea pig," Loretta said. "I don't think I can handle this."

As they discussed the procedure and the small likelihood of success, Jason watched the play of emotions across her strong face. He found himself empathizing in a way that was new to him. "You might want to talk this over with your husband."

After a brief pause, Loretta said, "He's left it up to me, and I have to face the fact that enough is enough." Tears sparkled along her dark lashes, but her chin came up in a gesture of pride. "Five years is a long time to ride a roller coaster. I want to focus on my other options and put this behind me."

Although Jason hated to see a patient give up, he knew sometimes that was the most sensible choice. "I'm sorry I don't have better news."

"At least you've helped me understand where the problem lies," Loretta said. "I'm grateful for that. Maybe I simply wasn't meant to have a child."

"Whatever you decide to do with your energies, I know you'll be terrific." Jason wasn't merely being polite. He'd come to admire her talents.

"Thanks. Well, the first thing on my agenda is planning next month's party to celebrate the fund drive, even though we're still five million dollars short." Loretta stood up. "It's going to be at the yacht club. I intend to organize a terrific bash."

"I'm looking forward to it," Jason said. As they shook hands on the way out, he knew she would triumph over this disappointment.

He had better news for his next patient, Eva Lo-Bianco, and her husband, Alfred. Despite the fact that only a dozen viable sperm had been retrieved from his specimen, the technique of injecting them directly into her eggs had resulted in three healthy embryos.

She clapped her hands excitedly. "When can you implant them?"

"We'll schedule the procedure right away," Jason said. "Congratulations and good luck."

Alfred shook his hand firmly. "We're glad to have this chance, Doctor. Our daughter is looking forward to having a baby brother or sister, and so are we."

"We'll do everything we can," Jason said.

He was rounding the corner toward the nurse's station when he came face-to-face with Heather. She put out one hand instinctively to brace herself. It molded itself to his chest, burning through the white lab coat.

Without thinking, Jason clasped her hand. It really did feel hot. "You aren't ill, are you? You might be running a temperature."

Heather shook her head. Her freckles almost disappeared into her flushed skin. "It must be the weather. It's warm for April."

"It might be warm if we were in Boston, but I understand sixty-degree temperatures are considered cool around here," Jason said.

She shrugged. "It's nothing. You startled me, that's all."

Jason no longer had to worry that she had taken leave due to some secret illness, now that he—and, thanks to Heather's new openness, the rest of the staff—knew why she'd really left. On the other hand, she'd proven herself very good at keeping secrets.

"Wait a minute." Jason couldn't let her go, not yet. "Your temperature's up? It's been three weeks since we were together. You aren't…"

He stopped in midsentence. A clinic hallway was no place to discuss the possibility that had just penetrated his brain.

They'd made love without using contraceptives. His throat constricted. What an idiot he'd been not to consider this earlier!

Despite his arrogant attitude about her nurse's situation, he himself had taken no precautions. And he'd been so preoccupied since their weekend together that the prospect of a pregnancy hadn't occurred to him.

Was there another baby on the horizon, a chubby-cheeked, button-nosed infant with her red hair and his green eyes? One that really would be his?

"No, I'm definitely not," Heather said flatly. "I'm sorry if this disappoints your desire to perpetuate your DNA."

"I wasn't thinking anything of the sort." What disappointed him most, Jason reflected, was that he had no excuse to get closer to Heather. A pregnancy would have forced the issue for both of them.

"You can let go of my hand now," she said.

He drew away reluctantly. "You're still annoyed with me."

"Whatever gave you that idea?" Despite her sarcasm, Heather didn't bolt. That, Jason hoped, was a good sign.

"The reference to perpetuating my DNA was my first clue," he said. "That was never my main concern. How's Ginger, by the way?"

"Happily settled in Texas." A wistful expression softened her briskness. "Olive and John are wonderful parents."

Not as wonderful as we would have been. Before he could voice this sentiment, Jason glanced past her to see Patrick Barr approaching with a clipboard.

"There you are!" The administrator closed in. "I need you to sign something." He held out the board, displaying an official-looking form.

"What's this?" Despite the mountains of paperwork he filled out daily, Jason insisted on examining each item carefully. He didn't recall seeing this particular form before.

"It's about Coral's probation," Patrick said.

"She's on probation?" He couldn't imagine what sort of crime a demure young woman like Coral could have committed. "For what, running a stop sign?"

A strangled noise came from Heather, as if she were suppressing laughter. "Not that kind of probation!"

"She doesn't become a permanent employee until you approve her," Patrick explained. "She's been with us for ninety days now. Is her job performance satisfactory?"

"It's fine." Taking the clipboard, Jason signed the form.

"Fine?" Heather asked. "That's all you can say?"

What did the woman want, a crash cart full of praise?

It wasn't Jason's style. "If I weren't happy with her performance, I wouldn't approve it."

"Everyone stand back." Patrick stretched his arms protectively. "I think we're in danger of being run down by our newest whirlwind."

Along the hall, head down and arms clamped around a stack of charts, barreled Alexei Davidoff. The blond doctor had a habit of charging from point to point that had resulted in more than one collision with other staff members.

"Excuse me," Patrick said as the man strode between them without looking up.

As if awakening from a dream, Alexei halted, blinked and studied them in momentary confusion. "Ah! I'm sorry, Dr. Barr."

"Call me Patrick, and it's no problem," said the administrator. "I'd been meaning to ask you how you enjoyed the mountains. At least, I assumed you were part of Jason's morale-boosting strategy."

Mentally, Jason gave himself a kick. He'd meant to confess all, or almost all, to the administrator weeks ago. Somehow it had fallen to the bottom of his to-do list.

Alexei gave him a puzzled frown. "Mountains?"

"I was going to explain about that," Jason said.

A nurse signaled the Russian doctor. "Have to go," he said. "Good to see you, Doctors."

As he disappeared down the hall, Patrick said, "Explain what?"

"The mountains," Jason said.

"Yes?" One eyebrow quirked questioningly.

"As it worked out, just Heather and I went," he said. "It was a very productive session."

"Productive?" Patrick asked.

Heather stood watching, saying nothing. Apparently,

she intended to let Jason dig himself into, or out of, a hole with no help from her.

"We ironed out a lot of problem areas, as I'm sure Dr. Rourke will confirm," Jason finished.

"You do seem to be getting along more smoothly," Patrick said. "Wasn't that a bit awkward, though, just the two of you?"

"We had a chaperone," Heather said. "My grand-daughter, Ginger."

"Glad to hear it." The administrator glanced from one to the other of them. "Whatever happened, it does appear to have been good for morale. Thanks for signing off on Coral's probation, Jason."

"My pleasure."

When they were alone again, Jason said, "I appreciate your backing me up."

Heather regarded him in a way that made his skin itch for her touch. Another moment and the rest of him would spring to full alert as well.

"I'm glad we're back on an even keel," she said. "You've kept your word to behave professionally."

That wasn't the reaction he'd hoped for. He would have preferred a subtle shifting of her body to throw her curves into prominence and a quick intake of breath, all of which would amount to a subtle invitation. Instead, he had to accept that she was perfectly satisfied with the status quo, even if it drove him crazy.

"Yes, well, I'm trying to do what's right." Jason finger-combed a rebellious shock of his hair. He could feel it spring back the moment he drew his hand away. "I'd better have Coral schedule a haircut for me."

"Pardon my saying so, but can't you schedule your own haircuts?" Heather said. "I don't know why that woman puts up with your high-handedness."

"I signed off on her probation, didn't I?" With a twinge of guilt, Jason reflected that Heather might be correct. Nevertheless, he wasn't the kind of person to tiptoe around his secretary's lack of assertiveness. "She needs to stick up for herself and not rely on me to read her mind. If she doesn't want to make my appointments with the barber, she should say so."

"She's timid by nature," Heather said.

"When I push, she has to learn to push back." Although Jason was willing to take some responsibility for getting along better with Coral, he had too much on his mind to cater to her insecurities. "I never have problems with Edith, you know."

"Anyone who tried to bully Edith would be lucky to escape with his life."

"That's fine with me," Jason said. "I'm not trying to dominate anyone."

"Oh? In my observation, you turn into a human bulldozer when you're in a bad mood," Heather said. More charitably, she added, "However, I suppose all doctors can be difficult at times, knowing we're responsible for life-and-death decisions."

"I wish Edith would give Coral some assertiveness tips," Jason said.

"Good idea." Heather smiled. "I might just suggest it."

He was about to ask her to have lunch with him when Heather's nurse summoned her to a phone call. Reining in his impulse to hang around, Jason returned to his office.

He didn't intend to stay away long, however. He'd made Heather smile today. Hope wasn't entirely lost.

THE UPHOLSTERED baby book, its cover trimmed in green and yellow and decorated with images of rabbits, already had one photograph slipped between its plastic pages: a wedding photo of Patrick and Natalie, who stood at an angle that revealed her growing abdomen.

''Trust my sister to pick that one!'' cried the honoree as she sat amid a pile of brightly colored wrapping paper on her sister Candy's sofa.

Heather smiled at her friend's high spirits. Natalie's natural optimism had often inspired her during the years since they'd become friends.

Around the small living room gathered co-workers and friends as well as some of Natalie's relatives. Baby clothes, bedding and toys lay unwrapped on the coffee table, along with a couple of unopened gifts. Almost everything at the baby shower featured a rabbit motif.

What if I'd gotten pregnant in the mountains? That idea kept popping up, despite Heather's attempts to focus on the festivities around her. She kept thinking that she, too, might have been welcoming a child into her life.

The longing had grown powerful in the days after her weekend with Jason. For a while, she'd half hoped she might be pregnant. She'd been stunned by the depth of her disappointment on discovering that she wasn't.

This eagerness for a baby wasn't practical, of course. Heather knew the difficulties of being a single mother and the disadvantages to a child of growing up without a father. Not that Jason would abandon her completely, but she doubted he'd be more than an occasional visitor. And eventually he'd be moving on to another job, out of state or out of country.

He apparently hadn't given the subject much consideration. When it had finally hit him last week at the clinic, he'd simply asked if she might be pregnant and accepted her answer with little sign of emotion.

Heather wanted to shake him. Didn't that man realize how special their weekend had been? She'd never known her body could experience such pleasure. And Jason had been a delightful companion, plopping himself into the snow beside her, building a fire, playing with Ginger.

Sure, she appreciated his respecting her desire for space. Yet a part of her couldn't help wishing he would pursue her.

Oh, why did she keep torturing herself? The one lesson she'd surely learned in all these years was that the only person Heather Rourke ought to rely on was Heather Rourke.

"Who brought this one?" Natalie reached for Heather's gift. "How cute!" She gave a little squeal as she pulled off the decoration, a tiny orange bunny attached to a thin elastic cord. "He's got personality."

"You can wear him on your wrist," Heather said. "I ordered a bunch of them as good-luck charms for my patients, kind of a lighthearted fertility symbol."

"I want one!" Amy said. "Although I don't require your services."

"How do you know you won't require her services?" Natalie asked. "Unless…" She broke off, her mouth open.

Noreen McLanahan clapped her hands together. "You've done it! You and Dr. Ladd are having a baby!"

"I wasn't going to announce it yet," Amy said. "I just found out."

"I'm thrilled for you." Heather gave her friend a hug.

She *was* glad for Amy. And hoped that someday she would know the same joy.

More congratulations poured in. It was a few minutes before everyone settled down enough for Natalie to unwrap the gift. Heather had assembled a group of appropriate children's books including *Pat the Bunny, Peter Rabbit* and *The Runaway Bunny*.

"I love these!" Natalie cried. "We'll enjoy them for years."

After the remaining gifts had been opened, they settled down to enjoying refreshments and conversation. Heather found herself too restless to stay for long, though, so as soon as seemed polite, she excused herself.

Next stop: the gym, to work off her excess energy. On a Saturday night, the place should be companionably busy. After fetching her gym bag, Heather drove directly there.

In the parking lot sat Jason's Mercedes. There was no mistaking it, due to the Doctors Circle parking permit on the windshield.

Maybe she should drive home and use the pool there, although it was dimly lit and probably deserted. No, Heather didn't intend to be chased away. Besides, a small part of her wanted to see Jason.

The only free parking space was beside the Mercedes. When she got out, Heather glanced through the window. In the back seat lay a couple of shirts obviously intended for the dry cleaners.

She knew instinctively how they smelled, of aftershave lotion and masculinity. And how they would feel, sliding against her skin as she undid the buttons. When she pulled the panels open, she would run her hands along Jason's chest, then press her breasts against his slight roughness.

At the thought, her nipples firmed into nubs and a flame sprang up inside her. She wanted to experience his

sheer physical potency all over again. She yearned to
watch the merriment in his eyes shade into searing passion.

Well, Heather had come to the health club to work
off her frustrations. Jason's presence had just added one
more, but so what?

Determined to give no sign of her longings, she tossed
the gym bag over her shoulder and marched inside.

Chapter Fourteen

As she approached the swimming pool, Heather's attention riveted on Jason. He was poised on the diving board, body tensed and arms clasped over his head, an arrow of pure masculinity. From his sculpted chest to his muscular calves, he'd been honed to perfection.

He sprang suddenly. The rear view as he arced downward was every bit as good as the front: broad shoulders, narrow waist, a taut butt. For a suspended moment, her spirits lifted and she flew with him until he flashed into the water.

Sharklike, Jason skimmed a dark trail beneath the surface. When he came up for air, Heather discovered that she'd been holding her breath.

An attractive blond woman had followed his progress as well. Circling toward him, she called out, "Well done!"

"Thanks." Jason lifted a hand in acknowledgement. Then he caught sight of Heather.

Their eyes connected with a spark that obliterated everything else from her awareness and, she believed, from his as well. If there'd been a bed close by, Heather didn't doubt that he'd have swept her to it. But only if she hadn't dragged him there first.

Hoping Jason didn't guess her reaction to him, she slipped off her thong sandals, padded to the pool's edge and lowered herself into the warm water. "You're quite a diver," she said as he swam to her.

The other woman dropped back, her expression disappointed but resigned.

"I was hoping you'd come here tonight," Jason said.

"I was at Natalie's shower." Heather felt the air vibrate between them. "After all that female bonding, I needed some exercise."

"Do you dive?" He shifted closer. With his damp hair pressed against his head. Heather could see how well-shaped his ears were, like everything else about him.

"Not well," she said. "I've always wanted to."

"I'd be glad to help," he said.

"Help me what?"

"Dive?" It was more of a question than a response. "Or did you have something else in mind?"

"No…" Yes, she did. What she had in mind was her and Jason, hot and eager, stripping off their swimsuits in her town house. They could make love in the queen-size bed that she'd bought three years ago but never shared with a man. Or in the living room, which was much too pristine and orderly now that Olive and Ginger had left.

Heather couldn't believe how much she wanted the man. Seeing him half-naked in his swimsuit reminded her of the way he'd brought her body to life that night in the mountains.

"If you'll get on the board, I'll show you," he said.

Heather did her best to stifle an unwanted image of

the two of them making love on the diving board. "Sure," she said. "A plunge in the drink will do me good."

Jason helped her out of the pool, his hand burning against her wrist. Heather was glad for the sake of discretion that she'd worn a one-piece suit, although it still revealed far too much of her breasts and hips for her peace of mind.

As for Jason's wisp of a swimsuit, it failed to hide the telltale sign of his arousal. As they walked the length of the pool, Heather felt his heat radiate around her.

She mounted the diving board. It gave her the sensation of standing much higher above the water than she really was.

"I have a fear of heights," Heather admitted.

"Heights?" Jason stood beside the board. He was so much taller that his face came to her shoulder. "You're not exactly on top of Mount Smoky."

"You forget that I'm accustomed to being very close to the ground," she said.

His teeth flashed white. "I'd prefer it if you were very close to me."

"I *am* very close to you." Her words came out barely above a whisper.

Jason nodded at a couple of swimmers staging an impromptu race across the shallow end. "If we were alone, I'd bring you even closer."

"Diving," Heather reminded him, and herself. "You were going to give me a lesson."

"Right." Gently, he guided her forward on the board. "Position your shoulders this way…"

It hadn't occurred to Heather that a diving lesson involved hands-on instruction. Very hands-on. Jason's grip moved along her waist and up her back, shifted to her arms, then to her hips.

Molten lava poured through her. She was sure that when she hit the water, it would hiss into steam.

Jason wasn't ready to let go yet. His deep voice kept murmuring instructions that sounded like endearments. Only when he spotted another would-be diver approaching did he give her the go-ahead.

Heather sprang forward. Propelled by a rush of energy, she soared higher than she ever had before and cut into the pool almost without a splash.

Behind, she heard the creak of the board. A moment later, Jason surfaced beside her.

"You're a good teacher," she said.

"You're a better student." He grinned lazily. "Somehow this exercise isn't wearing me out like it usually does. I'd prefer to find something more, shall we say, challenging." His tone left no doubt as to what kind of exercise he meant.

"You could use the rowing machine if you want to break a sweat," Heather teased.

"I can do that just looking at you."

Me, too. Although this rush of desire was delicious, she intended to fight it as hard as possible. "Maybe we should swim laps."

"If you want to." Easily, he stretched out in the water, matching his pace to hers as Heather chopped her way across the pool.

By the third lap, Jason was playing beside her like a dolphin. She had to chuckle at the man's antics. She didn't mind that he could swim circles around her, since she'd never claimed to be an athlete.

Her sensitivity to him flowed through her like warm

honey. The exertion cooled it slightly, but the sweetness remained.

After a while, Heather's muscles warned that it was time to take a break. When she said so to Jason, the two of them swam to the side of the pool.

"Up you go." Clamping his hands around her waist, he lifted her effortlessly. She enjoyed the freedom of being hoisted in the air, relying on him and knowing she could trust him. Even if it was an illusion.

A moment later, he landed beside her on the concrete and they headed out of the pool area. Heather hated parting from him, even to go change into street clothes and dry her hair.

This was crazy. She felt like a teenager, giddy and eager and fearless. She kept forgetting all the reasons why she was determined to keep him at bay.

They met back in the lobby, her in jeans and a turtleneck, him in jeans and a black shirt that ought to come with a warning that it was dangerously sexy. From the coffee shop wafted the scent of a snack that was a specialty of the house.

"I hate to mention it, but I'm hungry," Jason said.

"Me, too." Heather hadn't been interested in the sugary confections at the baby shower. Her tastes ran more to salty and sour than to sweet. No wonder she liked Jason, she thought ruefully.

They found a table overlooking the racquetball courts. Jason ordered a large serving of the specialty, which consisted of melted cheese and bacon bits on taco chips. They both dug in.

"I'd suggest we take this home except it might get cold," Jason said.

"We could microwave it."

"Cheese gets chewy in the microwave," he said.

"Picky picky!"

As he laughed, Heather's fingers bumped his on the plate. Ripples of anticipation shot through her. She almost suggested they forget the food entirely, except that it tasted so good.

"I'm glad we both had a free evening at the same time," Jason said. "From now until the gala, I'm not even sure when I'm going to sleep."

The event was scheduled for the weekend after next. "I didn't know you were that involved in the festivities," Heather said. "Or are you talking about your work schedule?"

"Mostly my work at the clinic." A trace of dark stubble showed on Jason's jaw when he turned to watch a rapid volley on the courts below. Heather smoothed her palm across his cheek and found the hair surprisingly soft. "You can do that again," he said. "And again and again."

"I just might." A few fellow diners were glancing their way, however, so she desisted. "I suppose we should act more dignified when we're in public."

"Only if we have to." Taking the hint, however, Jason leaned back in his chair. "You asked about my schedule. Well, you know how everything seems to pile up when you have the least time for it? I got word yesterday that Dr. Maurice Cocteau is arriving a week from Wednesday to check out our facilities, so I'll be showing him around."

"Why is he coming here?" Cocteau was the distinguished head of a French research facility outside Paris. Although Heather took pride in the Doctors Circle clinic, it was geared toward patient care, not research. She didn't see why Dr. Cocteau would take an interest in it.

"He's got some business in Los Angeles and figured he'd drop by as long as he's in the area," Jason explained. "I've run into him at conferences over the years and we keep in touch."

A warning bell sounded in the back of Heather's mind. "Are you sure he doesn't have an ulterior motive?"

"What possible motive could he have?" Jason spread his hands questioningly. "It's not as if he's going to find any techniques he can borrow. Although we may get innovative eventually, we've barely begun treating patients."

"I didn't mean that." In the day-to-day bustle of the clinic, it was easy to forget Jason's international reputation. He was a star, the kind that shone too brightly to be contained in one little corner of the universe. "He might want you to come work with him."

"I've made a commitment to Doctors Circle." Jason straightened in his chair, beginning to take her concern seriously. "I plan to stay for a while."

For a while. How long was that? Heather wondered. She knew that, eventually, Jason would be moving on, but she hadn't expected the issue to come up this soon. "What if he makes you the offer of a lifetime?"

"I can't run out on a responsibility," Jason said. "That wouldn't be right. It wouldn't be good for my reputation, either."

Was it her imagination, or did she detect a note of hesitation in his voice? If the offer of a lifetime came, Jason would have a hard time turning it down.

Of course, this was all speculation. Maybe Maurice

Cocteau simply wanted to visit an old friend while he was in the area, to touch base in case an opportunity came up at some later date.

Heather hoped so. For her sake, for their patients, for everyone they worked with.

But the conversation reminded her that, sooner or later, an irresistible offer was going to come Jason's way. And she knew that, when it did, he would accept.

He had to follow his heart. And she had to follow hers, which belonged right here in Serene Beach.

A rapid beep-beep roused her from her reflections. "Is that yours or mine?" Jason reached into his pocket.

Heather dug into her gym bag at the same time. "Mine," she said, reading the phone number. "It's Labor and Delivery."

"Can I take a rain check?" Jason said. "I'm assuming we were going to spend some meaningful time together tonight."

"We'd better wait." Heather felt as if she'd been saved by the bell. "Until things settle down."

"Until you're confident that I'm not planning to run off to Paris?" He'd obviously grasped what was running through her mind.

"Something like that." Heather spared him a regretful look.

"Heather, I can't help wanting to be the best doctor I can," Jason said. "That's who I am. But you're very special to me. I wish we could just enjoy the moment and let life take us where it will."

Heather's eyes stung with unshed tears. "I want that, too."

If only she could allow herself to enjoy this wonderful chemistry and this charming man for as long as it lasted, then say good-bye and never look back. At the age of thirty-six, she'd all but given up on marrying and having children, so why not?

Because despite everything she'd been through, her heart had never hardened. She was still vulnerable to loving too much and hurting too much afterward.

"If we both want the same thing, it's just a question of finding the right time," Jason said.

Heather drew back. "No, it isn't. I can't handle a love-'em-and-leave-'em guy, even if he's honest about it up front."

"Love 'em and leave 'em? I don't think of myself that way," Jason said.

"Maybe it sounds harsh, but it's the truth. Sorry, but this might be urgent." On her cell phone, Heather returned the call. When she clicked off, she said, "Cynthia's twins appear to be in a hurry. She's getting prepped for a C-section right now."

"I hope everything goes well," Jason said. "Tell her not to worry about her schedule when she gets back to work. We'll figure something out so she can raise those twins and be your nurse, too."

"Thanks." His kindness meant a lot.

Her throat constricting, Heather hurried out of the health club. She'd come perilously close to casting caution aside and taking what she wanted tonight. Maybe it would have been the best thing. At least she'd have another beautiful memory to look back on when she got old.

JASON LINGERED in the coffee shop, idly watching a man and woman battle each other on the racquetball court.

His body glowed from his exercise in the pool and from the building passion that hadn't yet diffused.

Heather had looked so adorable, he'd burned to take her home with him. She was not only utterly desirable but also his intellectual match, keeping pace with him verbally at every step. She was the kind of woman he would have dreamed of, if he'd been the sort of man to have romantic dreams.

In some ways she was very much like him, but in other ways, entirely different. Her patio garden summed it up: She put down roots. Even in his impulsive acquisition of a puppy, Jason had chosen something portable.

Why, then, did the room seem empty the moment she left it? Why did he ache for the sound of her voice?

A pager went off. This time, it had to be his, although he didn't have any patients likely to need emergency attention.

Jason checked it. He didn't recognize the number, but he dialed it anyway.

The voice that came on the line belonged to George Farajian. "I have a big favor to ask," said the head of the Ob/Gyn Department. "I'm on call this weekend but I took a golf ball to the head."

"Isn't it a bit late in the evening to be playing golf?" Jason asked without thinking.

George uttered a snort that sounded both humorous and painful. "It happened a couple of hours ago. I'm sitting at home with an icepack on my head and a bruise the size of a grapefruit."

He proceeded to outline the problem. Not only was Cynthia about to deliver her twins by C-section, but Rita Beltran, Loretta's sister, had just gone into labor with triplets.

As a specialist in complicated pregnancies, George was the best choice to perform the surgery. "Unfortunately, I'm woozy from painkillers. And with Heather tied up, there's no one on our staff as capable as you are," he said.

"Say no more." Jason grabbed his gear and sprang to his feet. "I'm on my way."

THE TWIN GIRLS came lustily into the world. Fully mature although a bit on the small side, they were as healthy as a mother could wish.

"Congratulations," Heather said, stitching up the mother while a pediatrician checked the newborns.

"Can I see them?" Cynthia asked from where she lay on the operating table.

"I'll have the nurse lay them next to you," Heather said. "As soon as they've had their tune-up."

A few minutes later, the first baby was set next to her mother while the second was being checked. Tears slid down Cynthia's cheeks, running past her oxygen mask. "She's so beautiful."

"You bet," Heather said. "Have you decided on names yet?"

After a long pause, Cynthia answered, "I'm not going to name them."

"Why not?" asked a nurse.

"Because..." The new mother stopped to clear her throat. "I've made a decision. Ever since you told me about giving up Olive for adoption, Heather, I've been thinking about it. I want Loretta Arista to adopt my babies. I know this is an unusual time to bring it up, but that's how I feel."

Silence fell over the operating room as everyone digested this unexpected information. "Have you talked to her about it?" Heather asked.

"No," came the reply. "But she and her husband would be perfect. I might even get to see the girls once in a while, although all I want is to make sure they're happy. Would you ask her for me?"

"I'll be glad to." Heather hoped Cynthia's decision hadn't been impulsive. Giving up a child for adoption, or two children in this case, was not a choice to make lightly.

From years of almost daily contact, Cynthia must have been able to follow her thoughts, because she added, "Don't put it off, thinking I'll take it back. I've talked this over with my counselor and given it a lot of thought. I'm not going to change my mind."

"I promise to talk to Loretta as soon as I can," Heather said.

What an unexpected situation, she thought, and what a wonderful opportunity for Loretta. Most would-be adoptive parents went through months or years of searching for a suitable child. But sometimes fate worked in mysterious ways.

Soon Cynthia, sedated to help the healing process, was moved to the recovery room, while the little girls were taken to the nursery. After cleaning up, Heather went to find out how Rita's delivery was going.

She wished she could have been there for this patient as well, but Cynthia had been prepped first. Besides, there was no one Heather trusted in an operating room more than Jason. She was glad he'd been available to fill in for George.

The delivery of triplets was a major production, re-quiring a large support team to take care of each child as well as the mother. According to the charge nurse, everything was proceeding well.

Cynthia went out to reassure Rita's extended family, who filled a large section of the lobby. Among them, she wasn't surprised to find Loretta and her husband, Mario.

"Could I talk to you both privately for a moment?" she asked after giving a progress report. "It's not about your sister."

"Sure." Wearing a puzzled expression, the public relations director and her husband followed Heather into the cafeteria. It was nearly empty at this hour and they were able to find a secluded table where no one would overhear.

"Maybe this isn't the best time to spring this, but I promised Cynthia I'd speak with you," Heather began.

"Oh, that's right, someone said she delivered her twins. Are they okay?" Loretta ran a hand through her dark hair. When it sprang back, the white streak stood out sharply.

"They're fine." Heather decided to get right to the point. "She told me on the operating table that she's decided to give up the girls for adoption and she wants you to have them."

Loretta blinked in surprise. Mario, a solidly built man in his mid-thirties with a down-to-earth air, began to smile. "Wow. Two little girls? I'll bet they're darling."

"I didn't think you cared whether we had children," his wife said.

"I didn't want to pressure you," he said. "But you know, all this business with your sister getting ready for triplets has made me think how much fun it would be to have kids."

"No one in my family has ever adopted," Loretta told Heather. "I wasn't sure I was comfortable with the idea, even though we went through the whole home study process."

"You're using the past tense. Does that mean you've changed your mind?" she asked.

"After seeing how happy Amy is with Quent's niece and nephew, I realized that once children belong to you, there's no difference," Loretta explained. "You love them the same as if you'd given birth to them."

Both of them had questions, of course. Over the course of the next half hour, Heather could see their excitement building. They decided to go view the babies at the nursery, then talk to Cynthia tomorrow when she'd be lucid enough for a discussion.

"If she really means it, we'll talk to an adoption lawyer on Monday," Mario said.

"You mean you're not going to leave the whole business to me this time?" teased his wife.

"Hey, I'm going to be a father." Mario put a companionable arm around Loretta's shoulders. "I plan to share the responsibility."

"Does that include learning to change diapers?" she asked.

"You bet."

A bittersweet sense of nostalgia twisted inside Heather as she watched them leave the cafeteria, talking eagerly together. This was the joy she'd handed to Olive's adoptive parents, although she hadn't completely understood it at the time.

She would never forget the pain of giving up her daughter. Mercifully, her emotions had mellowed now to an understanding of how much good she'd done for everyone. Above all, she was grateful that, in her case, life had come full circle and brought her a heaping measure of love.

Yet there was still something missing. Now that Ginger was growing up in Texas, far from her grandmother's constant attention, Heather missed having the chance to nurture a small child through every stage of development.

And she missed having a man to share the happiness. She still dreamed sometimes of a groom awaiting her at the altar as she strolled up the aisle. Would she ever find him?

In the lobby, Heather spotted Jason arriving to address Rita's assembled relatives. Although a bit rumpled after the operation, he was beaming.

"The neonatologist says the children are doing extremely well," he announced. "There are two girls and a boy. They're large for triplets and in excellent condition. We don't expect any serious complications, although they'll need to be watched closely for a while."

Excited relatives peppered him with inquiries, which he did his best to answer. In his white coat, Jason fit the image of a doctor that Heather had grown up with on television shows: strong, kind and confident.

More than that, he seemed genuinely thrilled as he discussed the children. There was such tenderness on his face that her resistance melted.

Across the lobby, his gaze met hers and he winked as if they were fellow conspirators. In a way, they were: both miracle workers.

Their paths were linked in so many other ways, too. If only their futures could be linked. Reluctantly,

Heather admitted to herself that Jason could easily be the man she'd dreamed about since she was young.

She loved him. There it was, clear and not at all simple. And, most likely, hopeless.

No matter how she felt, he would never be standing at the altar welcoming her into his future. He would never have a child with her that they could raise together. He had his own goals and they didn't include the kind of life she wanted.

To her dismay, Heather spotted him coming toward her. She froze. How on earth was she going to manage to act casually, after realizing that she loved him with all her heart?

Chapter Fifteen

"Is something wrong?" Jason asked. Up close, he looked even handsomer than he had across the lobby, although a bit tired, too, Heather mused.

Behind him, Rita's family streamed toward the elevators that led to the second-floor nursery. They'd have a field day viewing those three little sweethearts, even though the babies were still too fragile to be handled.

Heather shook her head. "It's just some old sentiments rising to the surface." She told him about Cynthia's decision to relinquish the babies.

Jason considered for a moment before responding. "Adoption may be a good idea for her, but I know it must be difficult. I hope it works out for everyone."

"You used to be more judgmental," Heather couldn't resist pointing out. "I remember you saying that she should have been more careful."

"That was before I, well, learned a few lessons of my own," he conceded.

"Such as what?"

"Such as what it's like to have a daughter. Even though I was mistaken." He released a long breath. "And let's face it, we weren't the least bit careful in the mountains. You were right about people getting carried away, even people who ought to know better.''

''Congratulations,'' she teased, ''and welcome to the human race.''

''Was I that bad?'' Jason's plaintive expression made Heather long to put her arms around him. She knew better than to do that, especially in the Birthing Center lobby.

''Sometimes,'' she said. ''I can be prickly, too, though.''

''Who, you?'' he joked. ''Never!''

''Only when pushed beyond human endurance,'' she amended.

They stood for a long moment, studying each other. Thank goodness the lobby was nearly empty on a Saturday night.

''I'm hoping we can continue this discussion at my place,'' Jason said. ''Or yours.''

A lump formed in Heather's throat. Now that she knew she loved him, she couldn't bear to risk her heart any further. ''Bad idea.''

''I'm sorry to hear that.'' He lingered for another moment, perhaps searching for words. What he finally said was, ''Then I'll see you at work Monday.''

''Great.'' Heather gave him a pleasant, impersonal nod. She maintained her composure all the way to the parking garage, where she sank into the front seat of her car with her pulse racing.

Had she made a mistake? Dr. Cocteau was arriving on Wednesday. Despite Jason's disclaimer, she had no doubt the French researcher was coming here with an agenda. And Heather had just made it clear that, as far as she was concerned, Jason could leave.

Well, so what? He wasn't going to stay in Serene

Beach on her account, in any case. One love affair more or less wouldn't stop the great Dr. Carmichael's relentless climb to international glory. Nor was Heather the sort of person to tag along with him, even if he asked her.

She'd made the right decision. She only wished the tears would stop rolling down her cheeks so she could put the car in gear and drive home.

ON WEDNESDAY morning, Jason got some terrific news. Eva LoBianco's home pregnancy test had come up positive. He repeated the test himself and got the same result.

"Congratulations," he told her and her husband. "Of course, it's very early but we can certainly be optimistic at this point."

"Can you tell how many babies I'm carrying?" she asked.

"It's too soon to tell," Jason said. "I'm afraid we'll have to wait about another month to do a sonogram. In the meantime, let's get you started with prenatal vitamins...."

After the patient left, he allowed himself a moment's jubilation. This was the first confirmed pregnancy for the clinic. Especially exciting was the fact that it had resulted from advanced technology.

Jason put in a call to Patrick Barr. The administrator let out a cheer. When he calmed down, he said, "Let's face it, it doesn't hurt that the father-to-be is one of Doctors Circle's benefactors."

"Good deeds sometimes bring their own reward," Jason said.

"Do you think it's too soon for a press release, assuming that they agree?"

"Way too soon," he said. "Let's wait until she successfully completes the first trimester." He had a good feeling about this one, though.

He was still elated when Maurice Cocteau arrived in midday. The physician, whose silver hair added to his distinguished appearance, inspected the premises with keen interest and congratulated Jason after hearing about the success with Mrs. LoBianco. He spoke politely with each other staff member to whom he was introduced, including Heather.

After the informal tour, they repaired for lunch to the Sailor's Retreat, a seafood restaurant beside the harbor. Through its broad windows, they had an expansive view of sailboats lazing in the sunshine.

"Southern California is very seductive," said the Frenchman as he perused the wine menu. "You are happy here?"

"Yes, I am." Jason knew the question hadn't been asked idly. Heather was right. The man had a proposition to make, although no doubt he intended to take his time about presenting it.

Maurice selected a sauvignon blanc. Jason decide to pass up the wine, since he wasn't used to drinking at midday.

They discussed new developments in reproductive research as they waited for their food. Jason was excited to learn about some of the work Maurice described at his facility near Paris.

"Your face lights up when we talk of these things," said his guest after they were served. "Yet you say that you are happy devoting yourself to clinical work."

"There isn't always a sharp distinction between clinical work and research," Jason pointed out. "As you know, often we discover things one step at a time, simply by adapting to circumstances.''

"This is true," the Frenchman agreed.

They both knew that, unlike the development of new medications, reproductive research was largely unregulated. Although doctors had to be careful for ethical as well as liability reasons, small advances in surgical and laboratory techniques could be made in a setting such as Doctors Circle.

"You have a great aptitude for research." Dr. Cocteau leaned forward, speaking intently. "Sometimes you must long to devote yourself to it without the pressures of scheduling so many patients and handling administration."

"No situation is perfect." Jason waited to hear what else his visitor would say.

"Naturally, I understand that you take your responsibilities here seriously, but surely by next year you can take a sabbatical to hone your skills," Maurice said. "We are prepared to offer you a three-month research fellowship next summer."

Jason hadn't expected this. A three-month stint at the French facility would enable him to keep up with the latest developments in research. He might even be able to make at least a small contribution of his own without requiring that he abandon his work in Serene Beach.

It would also mean temporarily leaving his patients in the hands of others. However, he was building a staff that would provide excellent care, and he'd be able to bring back new ideas that would benefit the whole program.

"It's certainly worth thinking about," he said.

"If you are happy with us, perhaps it will lead to other things in the future," Maurice said. "Who knows?" He downed a bite of his fish before saying, "The food here is very good. Not so good as in Paris, of course, but excellent all the same."

Paris. Jason, who had visited the city when he was working in England, loved the formal parks, sidewalk cafés and colorful flower stands. He missed the scent of the crisp loaves called baguettes drifting from the bakeries and the cultural offerings from the Louvre to the opera.

He would relish showing the city to Heather. Perhaps she might accept an invitation to visit him during his time away....

I can't handle a love-'em-and-leave-'em guy, even if he's honest about it up front.

But he wasn't planning to leave. There was nothing wrong with taking a sabbatical. Heather herself had gone on leave for two months last year.

"You're right about the food," he told Maurice. "And your offer is quite an honor. May I have a few days to think about it?"

"Of course," said his guest. "Take your time. Call me when you make a decision."

"It won't be long," Jason promised.

BEING INTRODUCED to Maurice Cocteau had been a memorable but also a deflating experience, Heather reflected that evening as she donned her oldest jeans and sweatshirt to wash her car.

The man radiated importance, not because of an inflated ego but because he was brilliant. She'd admired him for years. Yet, despite his courtesy, it had been evident that his real interest remained fixed on Jason.

Okay, so I'm not the whiz kid on the block, she told herself as she threw rags and a bottle of detergent into a bucket, draped a couple of old towels over her shoulder and picked up a footstool. I never have been. Why should it bother me now?

Heather let herself out of the town house, locked it and tucked the key into her pocket. Normally, she took her car to the local auto spa, which was what she'd done a few days earlier. Within hours afterward, she'd run into some mud generated by an overactive sprinkler, followed the next day by a close encounter with a couple of birds soiling her car. This time, she planned to give the vehicle a quick cleaning herself.

Twilight turned the landscaped walk into a jungle pathway. Perfume from a flowering vine reminded Heather that it was nearly summer.

As she circled the building toward her carport, she wondered what Jason was doing tonight. She'd like to find out what Dr. Cocteau had said. Maybe she should swing by his place....

If she intended to behave, she shouldn't seek out temptation, Heather rebuked herself. Besides, she was hardly dressed for socializing.

When she reached her car, she backed it out and drove a few dozen feet to where the manager left a hose coiled for the use of residents. In the gathering dusk, Heather set to work beneath a pole light while her mind resumed its earlier train of thought.

Was she jealous of Jason's prominence? Part of her had always been ambitious. Without that drive, she'd never have made it through medical school.

Heather tried to imagine what it would be like if Maurice Cocteau had come to Serene Beach to woo her instead of Jason. It would be flattering, but her strongest response was a sense of discomfort.

She wasn't some celebrity. She was a doctor who belonged with her patients, a woman who cared about her friends and a grandmother who didn't want to put any more distance then necessary between herself and Ginger.

The lights of an arriving vehicle flared by. Heather ignored it, too absorbed in soaping the car to care who might see her. It felt good to perform manual labor, even though she had to stand on tiptoe atop her stool to reach the roof.

She'd climbed down and was washing mud off the flaps when she heard masculine footsteps approaching. Jason.

The way his business suit outlined his broad shoulders sent a rush of desire through her. His shirt collar stood open and his tie was loosened, an open invitation for a woman to touch him.

This was not the way Heather wanted to react. Swallowing hard, she tried to act casual. "You're home on the late side."

"I had to make up for the time I took off at lunch," he said. "You know, the car ahead of me nearly drove into a wall because of you."

"Excuse me?" Heather hadn't noticed any cars until his. Subconsciously, she must have recognized the purr of Jason's engine.

"The guy got an eyeful of how you look in a wet T-shirt and nearly lost it," he said with a chuckle.

"This isn't a T-shirt." Heather glanced down. The damp sweatshirt threw her breasts into prominence, but she didn't know how anyone could have noticed when, for the most part, she'd been pressed against the car. "Guys must spend all their time ogling women's bodies."

"Don't underestimate yourself." Jason planted himself on the blacktop, his laptop in one hand. "And don't tell me women don't check out men's bodies, either."

"Yours is looking good," she said before she could stop herself.

His eyebrows rose. "Would you care for a closer inspection?"

"I'm kind of in the middle of something here." Heather indicated her car.

"I could change and come help you," Jason said. "As long as you promise we'll work very closely together."

The air crackled between them, the heat almost visible against the evening coolness. He was so much fun to be around, Heather thought.

And her arms would be so very, very empty when he went away.

"I enjoyed meeting Dr. Cocteau today." She adjusted the hose nozzle and began rinsing the car.

"We're moving on to that subject, are we?" Jason stepped back, protecting his computer. "Well, you were right. He made me an offer."

Heather nearly dropped the hose, grabbing it just in time to prevent a rather nasty mess. She doubted Jason would ever have believed she hadn't intend to douse him. "Oops. I mean, what kind of offer?"

"Are you licensed to operate that thing?" In the fading light, he became a powerful silhouette with an alluring voice.

"I haven't lost any bystanders yet," Heather said. "So did he try to hustle you off to Paris?"

"He offered me a three-month research stint next summer," Jason said. "It's only temporary. I wouldn't have to abandon Doctors Circle."

"It's a carrot." She hosed the last dribs of soap off the hood.

"A carrot?"

"Dangled on a stick." She wondered how long she dared let the car drip before attempting to dry it. It was a tradeoff: less work vs. more spots.

"Maybe so," Jason conceded. "Nevertheless, there's no reason I can't take leave occasionally. For one thing, it would add to the clinic's prestige."

"That's true." From a professional standpoint, Heather supposed her opposition to his accepting the offer might seem unreasonable. Surely Patrick had known when he hired Jason that the man was going to remain in demand.

"You'd like Paris," Jason said. "Ever been there?"

"Travel wasn't in my budget." When she was younger, Heather had dreamed of touring Europe, but paying for medical school had put it out of the question. "I guess I'll have to be satisfied with having toured the Paris Hotel in Vegas." The wedding party had eaten dinner at the replica Eiffel Tower.

"You could visit while I was on staff," he said. "Think of the educational value."

"Think of the gossip," she said.

"Are you going to let other people's nosiness ruin your life?" Jason asked.

"If I visited you for a short time, I wouldn't learn much," she said, avoiding a direct response. "And I couldn't stay long, because we'd already be short one doctor."

"I suppose that's true," Jason conceded. "But you shouldn't take it personally if I go."

"Why would I take it personally?"

"Because we have a relationship."

"That depends on your definition," Heather shot back. "The Hatfields and the McCoys had a relationship, too.'' She supposed that was a bit unfair, so she added, ''If we were truly in a relationship, we'd want to be together, not spend months apart.''

''It doesn't have to work that way.'' Jason seemed surer of his ground now. ''Lots of couples give each other elbow room. Look at Lisa Arcadian. She accepted a position here while her husband is working in Europe.''

''Someone told me they're separated,'' Heather said. It was amazing how fast stories had spread about the new staff members.

''I didn't know that. They're not a good example, then.'' He considered for a moment. ''Nevertheless, people don't have to be joined at the hip. With two professionals, it's inevitable for them to spend some time apart.''

Even if he was right, the problem was that, judging by Jason's past, he had a tendency to leave permanently when the going got tough. How could a woman be sure he'd ever come back? Heather wondered.

''I have nothing against travel or sabbaticals,'' she said, climbing onto the stool and applying a towel to the car's roof. ''It's a question of knowing where your roots are.''

''Some plants don't need roots,'' Jason shot back. ''They grow in the air.''

''Name three.''

''Name three what?''

''Three kinds of plant that grow in the air.'' Heather dried the side window in front of her.

''Horticulture is more your field than mine,'' he said.

''Well, I don't know of any,'' she said. ''I think it's an urban legend.''

"I'm not going to leave Doctors Circle any time soon," Jason told her. "But I can't promise to tie myself down forever."

"Who's asking you to?" Heather kept her face averted as she worked her towel around to the windshield.

There was a long pause, and then she heard him say quietly, "Frodo needs attention and I haven't eaten, so I'll bid you good night."

"Have a good evening," she called without turning.

"Did you mean…?" He stopped without finishing the sentence. "See you tomorrow."

Did she mean what? That she didn't want to be a dead weight around his neck? Sure, she'd meant it.

After his footsteps receded along the path, Heather muttered a few choice words about the poor quality of the overhead light. She could hardly see a thing.

Then she blinked, and discovered the problem wasn't the light. It was the tears clouding her vision.

BY FRIDAY MORNING, Jason still hadn't made up his mind whether to accept Dr. Cocteau's offer. He'd never had this much trouble making a decision before.

As he strode toward the clinic from the parking garage, he tried to picture himself in Paris. There was a rush of exhilaration, followed by a hollow feeling. The reason was unmistakable: He didn't want to lose Heather.

Perhaps he already had. She'd made it clear that she didn't want him sticking around for her sake.

She'd also said she didn't oppose the occasional sabbatical. Why, then, was she so upset about the possibility of his going to France for a few months? There was no reason that two professionals couldn't work out an arrangement without sacrificing their careers.

Jason needed the stimulation that came from surrounding himself with new opportunities and new people. At the same time, he could see how seductive it was to work in a clinic like this. Not only was it fulfilling to help couples create children but he felt a strong sense of loyalty to his less fortunate patients, who showed dedication and perseverance in the face of frequent disappointment. It would be all too easy to bury himself in the day-to-day details and lose sight of his goals.

Yet, more and more, he was finding it hard to imagine a future without Heather. He felt more truly alive in her company and more masculine than with any other woman he'd known.

He even had an absurd impulse to protect her, although she could obviously take care of herself. The other night, he'd considered borrowing the hose and washing the roof of her car, no doubt drenching himself in the process, so she wouldn't have to teeter on top of that footstool.

But he couldn't stop being who he was. To become less than his best, to lose his edge, would ultimately make Jason and everyone around him miserable.

As he entered the East Wing, Loretta bustled in behind him. She greeted him and pushed the elevator button to the second floor, which housed the administrative offices.

"You heard about my husband and me adopting Cynthia's twins, didn't you?" she asked, her face aglow.

"Heather told me," he said. "Congratulations. How's it going?"

If she'd grinned any more broadly, she might have

required plastic surgery. "It's wonderful. We may be able to take them home from the hospital in a few days."

"Your family must be excited, what with your sister having triplets and you adopting twins." He'd seen for himself last weekend what an enthusiastic crowd they were.

"You know what? My family astounds me," the public relations director said. "I wasn't sure how they'd react to my adopting, but they 'got it' right away."

"Got what?" Jason asked.

"The fact that I'm not settling for second best," Loretta said. "I simply changed my goal to do what was right for me. These little girls were meant to be Mario's and my daughters."

"I'm very happy for you," he said. "I only wish I could have done more."

"Please don't feel like you failed," she told him. "Maybe that advanced technique would have given me a baby or maybe not. It doesn't matter."

"Congratulations." Jason supposed it would have been nice to have another success story at the clinic. But this *was* a success story. "I hope you'll bring them to work sometimes so I can see them."

"Don't worry, you'll be watching them grow up," Loretta said as the elevator door opened. "See you later!"

"Good-bye." As he watched her go, Jason regretted that he probably wouldn't be around to watch those little girls grow up. Despite his resolve to stick by the clinic, that didn't mean forever. Loretta might be able to switch her goals and still find satisfaction, but Jason didn't see how he could.

He put aside his musings as he approached the nurse's

station. He was scheduled solidly all morning and his clients required one hundred percent of his attention.

It was after one o'clock by the time Jason came up for air. He still had a stack of administrative tasks to handle.

On the way into his office, he called to Coral, "Pick up a sandwich for me, would you? Corned beef on rye, please."

A small voice said, "Why don't you pick it up yourself?"

Jason nearly stumbled over his own feet. "What did you say?"

His secretary cleared her throat. "Fetching your lunch isn't part of my job description."

What on earth had gotten into the woman? Jason wondered. On the other hand, it wouldn't do him any harm to go to the cafeteria. The adjacent patio area was a restful spot where he could dine while reviewing paperwork.

"I've been wanting to try one of the pasta dishes anyway," he said. "I think I'll do that." From inside, he grabbed a couple of files, then headed out.

The import of what had happened didn't strike him until later that afternoon when he witnessed Edith giving Coral a high five. The chuckling nurse tried to pull a straight face when she spotted Jason, and failed.

What was the big deal? he wondered. His secretary had finally spoken up for herself, as she should have done long ago. It made life easier for everyone.

Jason managed to get caught up on his work by five-thirty. Other staffers were heading out, talking eagerly about the gala scheduled for tomorrow night.

The question of the day seemed to be, had the Endowment Fund met its thirty million-dollar goal? If not, how short had it fallen?

In the corridor, he passed Heather, who had flipped open a patient chart and was scrutinizing the contents. "Working late?" he asked.

"This is the last one," she said. "My client has a tough work schedule so I offered to stay till she could get here."

Jason had never doubted that the clinic would achieve an outstanding success ratio because of the staff's technical expertise. It struck him now that a contributing reason would be the flexibility and caring of his staff members, particularly this one.

"Good for you," he said.

"I hear Coral made a breakthrough today," Heather added with a trace of a smile. "She said no and lived to tell the tale."

"It shouldn't surprise anyone," Jason replied. "I've always said my bark is worse than my bite."

"You never said that!"

"That's because I prefer not to talk in clichés," he said. "But I implied it. My reputation as an ogre is highly exaggerated. Just ask Edith. She gets away with murder."

"Murder?"

"You wouldn't believe the things that woman says to me," Jason told her. "I don't mind. As I've always said, I demand outstanding work and dedication. I never asked for humility or blind obedience."

Heather closed the chart. "You know something? When Patrick hired you, I had to concede that your reputation was good for Doctors Circle and that there were techniques I could learn from you. What I didn't expect was leadership."

Jason hadn't given the subject any thought. "I'm doing my best to get things organized."

"More than that, you're setting the tone of the clinic," Heather said. "People admire you and they look to you for direction, including the other doctors. The nurses take pride in being assigned here. You're contributing more than you may be aware." With a grin, she added, "I would never have believed that, with your massive ego, you might actually underestimate your importance."

"I'm not sure whether to be flattered or insulted," Jason said.

"Good! I like to keep you off-balance." With a smile brilliant enough to light a thousand Christmas trees, she whisked away to her appointment.

Was she right about his leadership abilities? Jason had no idea. One thing he was certain about, however, was that there couldn't possibly be a woman, even in the beautiful and romantic country of France, whose smile could lift him three feet off the floor the way Heather's did.

Chapter Sixteen

Had she said too much or not enough? As she made a last-minute check in the mirror before heading to the Endowment Fund gala, Heather wondered whether Jason had already accepted the research offer from Dr. Cocteau.

He hadn't mentioned it yesterday, and she hadn't wanted to quiz him. In fact, she'd been in a generous mood after witnessing Coral's elation. She'd meant what she said about Jason's leadership abilities, whether or not it influenced his decision.

She had the uncomfortable sense that matters were going to come to a head this evening. There was no rational explanation for her premonition, except that an event like this sometimes encouraged people to make announcements of their own.

How would the other staffers react if Jason disclosed that he'd be spending next summer in Paris? They'd applaud and congratulate him, she supposed. They'd also probably speculate, as she did, that this might be the first step toward a departure.

Heather wrapped her arms around herself. In the full-length mirror, the gesture looked self-protective.

She was wearing the russet dress Jason had admired

at the boutique. During the festivities in Las Vegas, it had won plenty of compliments and interested glances from males, none of which had given her much of a thrill.

It was foolish, of course, to imagine that the gown cast enough magic to affect Jason's decision whether to stay at Doctors Circle. A man either loved you and wanted to spend his life with you, or he didn't.

Despite her carefully erected defenses, she'd fallen for Jason. Now she had to get over him. There was no sense in throwing herself at a man who would only break her heart.

Heather picked up her beaded evening purse. In her twenty-year struggle to rise above a youthful mistake, she had learned to keep her head high and never let the public see her vulnerabilities. That wasn't going to change even for Jason Carmichael.

She went forth determined to put a good face on whatever might happen.

DESPITE A busy day, Jason was one of the first guests to arrive at the Serene Beach Yacht Club. Although he'd driven past the Spanish-style stucco building several times, this was his first venture inside.

He was surprised to discover how large it was, sprawling along the harbor's edge. Outside, palm trees and a two-story parking structure had obscured its dimensions.

The blue-carpeted lobby opened into a dining room, a bar and an array of party rooms. Doctors Circle had reserved the ballroom, a glittering expanse with a wall of windows facing the water. After seeing the other men's formality, Jason was glad he'd worn the tuxedo he'd purchased in England.

An orchestra played in one corner, discreetly enough

not to drown out conversations. White-covered tables had been set up, although no food was being served yet. Champagne had been uncorked and punch flowed in a fountain.

Trying not to show how keyed up he felt, Jason shook hands with Patrick and inquired after Natalie. "She's occupied at the moment," the administrator said without elaborating.

"Did the fund drive reach its goal?" Jason asked.

"No comment." Patrick's expression gave nothing away. "Everyone's going to learn the facts at the same time."

"Trying to pry out the juicy details?" inquired Noreen McLanahan. The elderly board member-cum-volunteer sparkled with diamonds shown to advantage by a black silk pantsuit. "This man's full of secrets tonight. He's promised us lots of surprises. Oh, Dr. Carmichael, have you met my beau, Hugo Oldham?"

"I haven't had the pleasure." He shook hands with the balding, tuxedoed man on her arm.

They were soon joined by Alfred and Eva LoBianco, both radiant. Gradually, the room filled with people. Heather hadn't arrived yet.

Jason hoped she wasn't going to prove difficult tonight. He'd made his decision and, although it had come at the last minute, it didn't feel rushed because it had been building inside him for a long time. Now that he'd made it, he didn't know why he'd ever hesitated. He just hoped that she would trust him.

When she entered the ballroom, Jason felt a shimmer in the air. A moment later, he spotted her near the entrance.

As he made his way toward her, he drank in the high color on Heather's cheeks and the gown with the scarf he'd picked out. She might have strolled right out of a dream. In fact, she had appeared in one of his dreams wearing that dress, but she hadn't kept it on very long.

"May I have this dance?" He offered his arm when he reached her.

Heather hesitated. "Oh, go on!" said her friend Amy, who stood nearby.

"I'd be delighted." Laying her hand on the sleeve of Jason's tuxedo, Heather glided beside him to the dance floor.

Gazing down at her hair, he saw that the curls framed her face softly. Her airy fragrance floated in the air.

It was a good beginning, Jason reflected. He just hoped her good mood wasn't going to give way to an explosion later on.

THE TUXEDO did a magnificent job of showcasing the man. Heather barely managed not to melt right into Jason's arms.

She had no idea what the orchestra was playing or who else had showed up at the party. The only thing she noticed was Jason's hand branding itself onto her waist as he guided her around the dance floor.

Despite her high heels, Heather's cheek only reached to his broad chest as they moved to a slow number. She imagined she could hear his heart beating.

She flashed back to the week after his arrival, months ago, when she'd imagined his heart had formed of green ice. How much she'd learned since then!

There was nothing cold about Jason Carmichael. He blazed against her, surrounding her with warmth. His mouth brushed the top of her head and she heard him murmur an endearment.

Longing flooded Heather, to be alone with him, to hear him tell her that he loved her and wanted to be with her always. What an idiot she was!

She forgot her reservations as the music swelled. Jason was a skilled dancer and Heather floated, leaving reality behind as she let him carve a path through space and time.

Beneath his tailored clothing, she felt the masculine hum of energy. Desire hovered just out of reach, like a promise not quite ready to be fulfilled.

When the song ended, they stayed where they were, ignoring the other people on the dance floor. Through the windows, Heather saw that darkness had completed its descent. Lights twinkled from moored yachts and the Serene Peninsula curved like a half-moon across the bay.

"Heather." Jason's breath tickled her ear.

"Mmm?"

"Later, I'd like to talk to you privately," he murmured.

A tiny flame of hope lit within her. "I'd like that, too."

"There's something I have to explain," he said.

The flame flickered and died. No explanation was necessary for a declaration of love. He must have decided to accept Dr. Cocteau's offer. Heather's throat clamped shut, cutting off any reply.

"Ladies and gentlemen." In front of the now-silent orchestra, Patrick had taken the microphone. "I'm sorry to interrupt the fun, but I've got a few things to say."

Everyone gathered closer. Jason kept one arm around Heather's waist. She hoped she could hear Patrick's remarks through the tumult in her brain.

To one side, she noticed Loretta answering questions from a young woman with a tape recorder and a pad.

Nearby, a cameraman took aim at Patrick. The local press, she gathered.

"As you all know, this gala celebrates two major events," the administrator continued, his voice ringing out and his manner relaxed. "The first is the opening of the Doctors Circle Infertility Clinic. If anyone hasn't met him yet, I'd like to introduce its director, Dr. Jason Carmichael."

Jason waved one hand in response. He blinked in surprise as cheers filled the air. The man had probably never been popular before, Heather thought. Well, he'd earned it.

After providing some background on the staff, Patrick went on to cite the nine-month-long Endowment Fund campaign. "Although Doctors Circle is on sound financial footing, we're banking on the fund to assure our future," he said. "By raising thirty million dollars, I hoped we could both guarantee the continuation of our current programs and support future expansion."

"Did we make it?" someone called.

"Here's the tricky part," Patrick said. "Bear with me a minute." He recounted the kickoff campaign last fall, Alfred LoBianco's generous donation, the ten million dollars raised in matching funds, and other contributions from the community.

"As of last week, we found ourselves still five million dollars short," he said. "If we couldn't make up the difference, we would also lose five million dollars in matching funds."

The room went quiet. Heather could feel the tension in Jason's encircling arm. Apparently he cared about Doctors Circle despite the likelihood that he wouldn't be staying very long.

"Our center has an angel," Patrick said after a long

moment. "Her name is Noreen McLanahan. She and some of her friends, including Mr. Hugo Oldham, have come up with the money. I'm pleased to announce that the Endowment Fund has met its goal!"

The room shook with shouts and applause. Standing to one side, Noreen blushed and Hugo ducked his head.

Jason was hurrahing along with the best of them. For this moment at least, he stood together with his fellow staff members, sharing their triumph.

Heather added her applause to the din. She'd suspected that, one way or another, Patrick would find a way to raise the money even if he couldn't do it within the prescribed time period. Still, she was proud of him and grateful to everyone who'd contributed.

Doctors Circle, the place she loved and considered home, was now solid as a rock. Women could continue to receive the care they needed regardless of their financial situation. Babies born in Serene Beach would come into the world as safely as possible.

Patrick held up one hand to stop the cheering. "I have one more announcement to make."

Heather went cold. Was he going to tell them about Jason's receiving the honor of an invitation from Dr. Cocteau?

"Actually, I have two announcements," Patrick said. "The first is that, having achieved my goal of putting Doctors Circle on sound footing, I plan to step down as administrator as soon as a replacement can be found."

A shock wave ran through the room. Faces went white. "He can't do that," Jason said. "We all depend on him."

Heather was tempted to point out that that was how his staff members felt about Jason as well. She couldn't, though. She was too distraught.

How could the center lose Patrick? He was not only the man who'd rescued it from the incompetence of his predecessor, he was also a father figure to all of them.

"I won't be going far," Patrick said. "I've decided to resume my pediatric practice and I'm going to do it at Doctors Circle. As you know, Dr. Dudley Fingger has been filling in as temporary head of the Well-Baby Clinic. Dudley has indicated he'd like to spend more time with patients, so, if the board approves, I'm going to appoint myself to that position."

Murmurs of approval and relief rolled back at him. At least he'd still be around, Heather thought. If the new administrator didn't measure up, he or she would no doubt find Patrick riding herd.

"Now, on to my second announcement," he said. "This is more personal. My wife Natalie isn't with us tonight because she went into labor a short time ago. Is there a doctor in the house?"

Amid the laughter, Heather said, "I think that's my cue."

"Call in and see how far along she is." Jason wasn't eager to let her go, she was pleased to find. "This is her first baby. She might not need you for hours."

Heather dialed Labor and Delivery. The charge nurse, who was keeping close tabs on Natalie's progress, told her labor was progressing quickly.

"She's asking for you," the nurse said. "I think it's a good idea for you to come in now."

"I'll be right there." Heather rang off. "I've got to go."

"You'll make quite an impression, dressed like that." Jason indicated the sleek gown.

"I keep a change of clothing in my office," she said.

"New office or old office?"

Heather didn't see what difference it made. "The old one. I haven't moved everything yet. Darn! The building's probably locked." Although the Birthing Center operated twenty-four hours a day, that wasn't true of the office buildings.

"Patrick has a passkey. I'm sure he's heading that way himself." Jason strode over to the administrator, who nodded and spoke into the microphone again.

"Everybody have a good time and party as long as you like. I'm going to be with my wife," he said. "Loretta Arista's in charge of the festivities in my absence. She's prepared a press release about the fund-raising campaign and my stepping down, and will answer any further questions."

As he moved toward Heather, Amy said from nearby, "I'll call Natalie's mother."

"Thanks. I'd forgotten to do that." Patrick came abreast of Heather. "Well, Doctor? Let's go see about our patient."

She spared one last, wistful glance at Jason, who gave her an encouraging thumbs-up. It would have been fun to dance with him some more, Heather thought. Heaven knew when they'd get the chance again.

It wasn't as if he was leaving right away, she told herself. They'd have plenty of time to talk. She just wasn't sure what they were going to talk about.

MELISSA ASHLEY BARR weighed seven pounds, four ounces. She had her mother's blond hair and blue eyes, and her father's gift for playing to an audience. As Patrick held the baby up in the nursery, Heather could have sworn Melissa smiled at her grandmother and assorted relatives and friends, although the infant was much too young for such interaction.

"I've examined a lot of babies in my time," Patrick said, turning away from the glass with his daughter in his arms. "I've never seen one who was such a ham before. Have you?"

"Absolutely not." Heather refrained from mentioning that Ginger had also been a shining example of infant perfection. There was no such thing as objectivity when it came to one's offspring, she supposed. "Are you going to stop back by the gala?"

"I'll let them manage without me, but you go ahead," Patrick said.

"Thanks." Heather went to strip off her protective clothing. She was tired after several hours at the Birthing Center, handling not only Natalie's delivery but also that of another patient.

Was Jason still at the yacht club? Even though she wasn't eager to hear his bad news, Heather hated to give up this chance to spend time with him. It wouldn't hurt to swing by and have a bite to eat, she told herself.

Eagerness speeding her step, Heather returned to her old office and changed into her evening dress. She was picking up her purse when the cell phone rang inside, making her jump. What timing! she mused as she answered, "Dr. Rourke."

"Dr. Carmichael here."

Her pulse speeded at his deep, familiar tones. "Natalie had a baby girl. You can tell everyone at the party."

"I'm not at the party," Jason said. "I had to leave on some business of my own."

Her spirits took a nosedive. "I guess there's no point in my going back, then."

"Actually, you could do me a favor if you don't mind," Jason said. "I left an envelope on my desk that I'm going to need first thing in the morning. It's marked

Urgent. I'd appreciate it if you could bring that home with you and leave it on my doorstep."

What on earth could he need urgently on a Sunday morning? Heather didn't like to pry, however. Besides, another problem had occurred to her. "The building must be locked."

"I called Patrick and he said he'd leave the side door open, the one near my office," Jason said.

"You think of everything."

"I do my best." He sounded pleasant but a bit preoccupied.

It irked Heather that he wasn't as bothered as she was that they'd lost the chance to dance some more that night. Trust Jason to be the most unromantic man on earth!

"Okay, I'll pick it up," she said. "I'll drop it at your town house."

"Great!" Jason said. "This means a lot. Oh, one more thing. Would you call me when you pick up the envelope? I think it's on my desk but there's a possibility I stuck it somewhere else."

"If it's not there, I'll call."

"Call either way," he said. "I can't tell you how important this is. Humor me."

What was going on? Heather felt as if they were playing some kind of game, but surely the great Jason Carmichael didn't stoop to practical jokes. "Fine. I'll call."

"Do you have my number with you?"

"Give it to me again." Heather had no intention of letting Jason know she'd programmed his cell number into her phone. His ego was big enough already.

After reciting it for her, he signed off with, "Talk to you in a few minutes."

Heather grumbled to herself as she went outside, setting the door to lock behind her. Did the man have any idea what time of night it was? He ought to do his own fetching and carrying. No wonder Coral had staged a palace revolt!

She smiled to herself, remembering the secretary's elation yesterday after she'd refused to fetch Jason's sandwich. The fact that the doctor had accepted her refusal without comment had made the point more clearly than either Edith or Heather could. Being assertive was not going to harm Coral's career.

She crossed the courtyard beneath a bright May moon. A couple of pole lights cast their glow across the silent fountain and empty seats. At one end of the plaza, the illuminated Birthing Center pierced the darkness.

Inside, new mothers were dozing and babies were staring around at their brand-new world. What a magical place, she thought.

The side door to the East Wing opened easily. Heather was glad to find the corridor lighted. Patrick must have flipped a switch when he unlocked the place earlier.

Jason's office was lit up, too, she found. There on the desk, as promised, sat an envelope marked Urgent. It was thick and oddly weighted, she discovered when she picked it up. There seemed to be a small object inside.

Remembering her instructions, she rapid-dialed Jason's number. "What's this all about?" she asked when he answered.

"What's what all about?" His tone of mock innocence failed to reassure her. "Oh, before you leave, you might want to look in your office. The new one."

Although Heather was tempted to try to pin him down, it would be faster to comply. Whatever game was afoot, no doubt she'd find the answer at the far end of the hallway. "Fine. Do you want me to call you when I get there, too?"

"It will be self-explanatory," he said. "See you later." Click.

Whatever Jason had planned, he'd gone to a lot of trouble. Her curiosity fully aroused, Heather marched along the corridor. If she hadn't been wearing high heels, she might have broken into a trot.

Chapter Seventeen

Reaching her office, Heather opened the door and found the room dark. As she reached for the light switch, she inhaled a perfume so fresh it might have come from...

...a whole bank of roses. As the room sprang to life, she saw bush after bush, each in full bloom, the containers swathed in colored foil. Arranged on tiers of portable stands, they transformed her office into a garden.

"I hope you like them." Jason moved into view. From the proud carriage of his head to the straightness of his back, he looked every inch a man in charge.

"What's going on?" she asked.

"Look in the envelope."

Heather tore it open. Out fell a key, which she managed to catch, and a note. Her hands were trembling so hard it took two tries to unfold it.

Across the paper slashed Jason's bold handwriting. "This is to unlock our house. It's a blank key because we're going to choose the house together."

"A house?" The words stuck in her throat. Heather's brain was stuck, too. She couldn't absorb all this, or perhaps she didn't dare to.

"Complete with roses," Jason said. "Isn't that what you had in mind?"

Was this his way of placating her so she would accept a relationship on his terms? ''Not if it's only temporary.''

''Who said it's only temporary?''

''On Wednesday, you were talking about needing elbow room and how plants can grow in air,'' she said.

Jason shifted toward her. ''I was raised to believe that my worth depended on my accomplishments. And those accomplishments had to be external, out there for the world to admire. I admit, it's taken me a while to realize that that's not what's really important.''

''What *is* really important?'' Heather scarcely dared to breathe.

''I guess I need to explain, since I haven't prepared you for this very well,'' Jason said. ''You see, something was holding me back from accepting Dr. Cocteau's offer. I didn't realize what it was until I read this morning's newspaper.''

Had he accepted the offer or hadn't he? Heather tried to speak, and found her throat too clogged. *Please let him say the right thing. Please don't let this be his way of buying me off.*

''I came across a story about an old mentor of mine,'' Jason continued. ''He died in his sleep at the age of eighty-five.''

She mouthed the words, ''I'm sorry.''

''I always wanted to be as much like him as possible,'' he said. ''As I read the article, I kept thinking that my accomplishments would never measure up to his. Then I reached the bottom. It said he'd been divorced twice and left no surviving family.''

''How sad.'' Heather hoped the man had had close friends.

Jason reached out to touch her arm. ''I kept wondering

who was at his bedside. I realized I don't want to end up alone without you, no matter how much glory I reap along the way. I want us to be a family.''

A family? Did he mean that?

''A lot of things came together all at once.'' Jason said. ''I couldn't believe I hadn't grasped it earlier. Being with the woman I love, working surrounded by people I care about, is just as important as changing the world. Because, in a way, this is the world. This is *my* world.''

''Mine, too,'' Heather whispered.

''Once I understood that, I couldn't bear to wait another day,'' he said. ''I kept remembering how much you wanted roses and this idea popped into my head.''

''About buying a house?'' she managed to ask.

''Not just the house…'' A quizzical look replaced his cheerfulness. ''Did I leave something out?''

''I don't know. Did you?''

He gave a brief wave of the hand as if impatient with himself. ''Let's back up. I can't believe I omitted the most important part.''

''Should I go out in the hall and come in again?'' Heather asked, only half kidding.

''That won't be necessary.'' Jason made a small embarrassed noise in his throat. ''The point I've been trying to make in my clumsy way is that I love you. Heather, will you marry me?''

The joy inside her was too pure, too precious to savor all at once. With what remained of her self-possession, she said, ''I've always imagined that when a man proposed to me, he would kneel.''

Jason's green eyes sparkled at her. Why had she ever thought them icy? ''Is it one knee or both knees?''

''Either way.''

With more grace than she'd expected, he lowered himself to one knee. In his tuxedo, he put her in mind of an English lord, proposing to his lady in a rose garden.

"Will you marry me and make your home with me, Heather?" he asked. "I want to spend the rest of my life with you. I'm ready to put down roots and I hope you'll show me how."

Tears stung her eyes. How could her dream be coming true, when she'd long ago given up on dreams?

"I thought I was going to lose you. I figured you wanted to talk to me privately to tell me you'd accepted Dr. Cocteau's invitation," she confessed.

"I gave him my polite regrets. I hope you're not about to do the same."

Heather couldn't believe the arrogant, hard-driving Jason Carmichael was speaking like this. As she studied his face, so full of hope, she knew that whatever she decided right now would determine the course of their lives. Either she retreated into a protective shell or she risked her heart by giving it without reserve.

"No." Seeing his expression cloud, she hurried to explain, "I mean, no, I'm not about to give you my regrets. The answer is yes. I love you, too. I have for a long time."

In a flash, Jason regained his feet and pulled her to his chest. "Say that again."

"I love you...."

She didn't get to finish. His kiss drove the words away.

There was a new sweetness to their embrace. When he stroked her hair and touched her cheek, Heather experienced a joy that swept away all the sorrows and doubts of the past.

She realized that having a house and roses no longer mattered so much. With Jason, Heather had come home, and with him, she was going to stay there.

THEY MADE LOVE in the bed she'd bought for herself and never before shared with a man. This, she mused as they lay together afterward, was what the bond between a man and a woman was meant to be.

It had certainly been a night to remember. Doctors Circle had raised thirty million dollars to ensure its future. Its nursery was filled with healthy babies. And Heather had found the one thing that had been missing despite all the other wonderful parts of her life.

She nestled against Jason's shoulder, inhaling the tangy essence of him, trusting at last that he would always be there. "I want to hear my favorite part again," he said.

"What's that?"

"The part where you tell me you love me." He brushed a kiss across her hair.

"That's my favorite part, too. I mean, when you tell me."

"Let's do it together. I'll count one, two, three…"

"Jason!" Heather couldn't believe he was acting silly at a time like this."

He laughed. "I love you, Heather."

"I love you, too."

"That felt good," he said. "You know, I wasn't sure how you'd react to my proposal."

"You must have had some clue," she pointed out, drawing the covers around them. "Otherwise you took quite a risk, stocking my office with roses."

"It was worth looking like a fool," Jason murmured. "I'd have been a bigger fool if I didn't try. As a matter of fact, I had no intention of giving up easily. By now, you must know how tenacious I can be."

"I can picture you running around all day, buying roses, setting them up, figuring out that business with the key," she said. "It was quite a production."

Jason chuckled. "The hardest part was going to be luring you away from the ceremony. Natalie's labor turned out to be very convenient."

"It wouldn't have been so convenient if I'd had to stay at the Birthing Center all night!"

"I'd have waited," he said.

"But you hate wasting time," Heather blurted, sitting up straight so she could look at him.

"It wouldn't have been wasted." In his eyes, she saw a new maturity and a new devotion. "It would be the most worthwhile time I ever spent."

Moisture blurred her vision. "I'm so glad you didn't let me discourage you." Mischievously, she added, "Does this mean I can expect you to be patient from now on?"

"Actually, no," Jason said. "To begin with, I don't believe in long engagements. How does a June wedding sound to you?"

A month wasn't much time to find her ideal dress and arrange for a church full of flowers. But those things didn't matter as much as they used to, now that Heather had won the man she loved. "It sounds terrific."

The next thing she knew, Jason was kissing her again. It seemed a shame to stop there, so they didn't.

Two months later

"THIS IS the one," Heather said the minute she stepped onto the patio.

"You haven't seen the upper floor yet," the real estate agent pointed out.

"I guess she doesn't need to," Jason said.

Wordlessly, Heather gestured at the slope behind the house, enjoying the sparkle of her diamond wedding ring in the July sunlight. She'd known all along what she wanted, and now she'd found it.

They'd visited several homes in this new hillside tract, each charming in its own way, but the small yards, mostly taken up by steep rear banks, hadn't offered her much scope for gardening. This one was different. Terraced, the slope offered row after row of possibilities, although at the moment there was nothing but bare dirt and a few weeds.

Heather pictured tiers of roses, much like the magical effect Jason had created in her office. The bushes, which had been perfuming her town house's courtyard for several months now, would fit perfectly here.

The real estate agent didn't argue. "Just to fill you in, there are three more bedrooms and two baths upstairs. Do you have children?"

"No, but we have a grandchild." Jason kept his expression deadpan. It was typical of him to let the woman try to figure out for herself how that was possible.

They'd seen Ginger last month when she, Olive and John had flown into town for the wedding. The little girl was crawling already, and she'd obviously missed her grandma.

They'd been married at the Serenity Fellowship Church next door to Doctors Circle, in a ceremony attended by Jason and Heather's immediate families along with a crowd of their fellow staffers. Afterward, they'd all enjoyed dinner and dancing at a hotel near the beach.

Heather didn't remember ever attending a party with so many babies. Natalie had brought little Melissa, Rita had attended with her triplets and Loretta with her twin girls. Cynthia had sat with them, treasuring the infants she'd relinquished while discussing her plans to enroll in a master's degree program.

There were lots more babies to come among the patients at the Infertility Clinic, with new success stories every day. The furthest along was Eva LoBianco, now in her fourth month and already decorating her nursery.

Amy, too, was experiencing a healthy pregnancy. Although Heather missed being able to care for her friend, since she no longer handled non-infertility patients, she knew Rob Sentinel was doing a fine job.

With so much going on, she and Jason had taken only a brief honeymoon in San Francisco. However, they planned a two-week trip to Europe in the fall.

"Spend as much time looking around as you like," the Realtor said. "If you decide to make an offer..."

"Give us a minute, will you?" Jason asked.

"Sure thing." The woman went inside.

Heather couldn't wait to make her case. "It's fenced, so Frodo can have room to stretch his paws." The puppy had grown in the past few months and was becoming rambunctious, although Jason trained him diligently.

"I can see why you love the place." He reached out to ruffle her hair. Heather loved when Jason touched her in small ways, which he did often. "It suits me, too. Let's go for it."

Gazing at the grounds of their future home, she nodded agreement. During the past two months, she and Jason had grown closer in a thousand ways. They worked together and played together and, on Sundays, he fixed her breakfast in bed. Now they'd found their house, too.

There was just one thing missing. But not for long.

"We haven't looked into the school district yet," Heather said.

"The school district?" Jason asked.

"I suppose a man who expected Ginger to attend kindergarten at a middle school wouldn't pay attention to such things, but I prefer to look at the teacher-to-student ratio and the curriculum," Heather said. "We want our child to get the best start possible."

"Our child." He repeated the words reverently. "Does this mean what I think it does?"

She'd barely managed not to shout the news the previous day after administering her own pregnancy test. "I was saving it for the right moment. This seems to be it."

"You mean you're...we're going to have... Wow!" With a shout, Jason grabbed Heather and swung her in a circle, then lowered her with a worried expression. "Did I hurt you? Do you feel all right?"

"I'm fine." She laughed. "As a doctor, you know a little excitement isn't going to hurt me."

"It's different when it's my own wife," he admitted. "I guess I'm going to be one of those husbands who shares the whole pregnancy."

"That should be quite an experience!" Heather laughed. "And just think. We didn't even need a petri dish."

Jason gathered her gently against him. "We must be the two luckiest people in the world."

For once, she didn't argue.

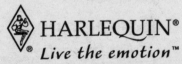

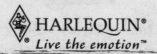

If you enjoyed what you just read,
then we've got an offer you can't resist!

Take 2 bestselling love stories FREE!

Plus get a FREE surprise gift!

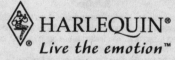